# STEALING
# KEVIN'S HEART

A NOVEL

**M. SCOTT CARTER**

THE ROADRUNNER PRESS
OKLAHOMA CITY

Published by The RoadRunner Press
Oklahoma City
www.TheRoadRunnerPress.com

First edition hardcover, The RoadRunner Press, October 2011
Printed in the United States of America.
Cover photo by Darren Parker, McNeese Fitzgerald Associates
Design by Jeanne Devlin

Published October 12, 2011

Library of Congress Control Number: 2011927843

Publisher's Cataloging-in-Publication
(Provided by Quality Books, Inc.)

Carter, M. Scott.
    Stealing Kevin's heart : (a young adult novel) / M.
    Scott Carter. — 1st ed.
    p. cm.
    SUMMARY: After losing his childhood friend in a
terrible accident, Alex, the star athlete, blames
himself. He becomes depressed and suicidal. When his
parents send him to a special camp for troubled teens,
he meets the perfect girl. She also holds the key to
dealing with the loss of his friend.
    Audience: Ages 12-18.
    LCCN 2011927843
    ISBN-13: 978-1-937054-05-2

    1. Teenagers—Juvenile fiction. 2. Heart—Infections
—Transplantation—Patients—Juvenile fiction. [1. Grief
—Fiction. 2. Teenagers—Fiction. 3. Heart—Infections
—Transplantation—Patients—Fiction. 4. Grief—
Fiction.]   I. Title.

PZ7.C24624Ste 2011          [Fic]
                      QBI11-600098

*For Karen, the girl who stole my heart*

# STEALING KEVIN'S HEART

# PROLOGUE

LIFE SUCKS. THE WHOLE world, everything, bites. I don't care if I ever wake up. I don't care about school—I haven't been in days. And I could care less about my little sister, Jenny, or her dumb piano recital. Then there's Bill—he's been planning some lame family trip for months now—well, screw him.

I'm not going.

Life sucks—in stereo.

It didn't used to.

It most definitely does now.

Take today. I'm trapped in the car with my stupid sister and Bill and Clarise (my parents, in case you're wondering). We're driving home on this stupid, rainy day past the synagogue where we just spent two hours listening to a stupid, bald guy in a rumpled dark suit, with a beanie-thing on his head, go on and on about all this religious mumbo jumbo that I care nothing about.

I told both Bill and Clarise yesterday that I wasn't going.

I spelled it out clearly: *I did not want to go.*

Did they listen to me? Not hardly.

They made me go. My life is bad television.

*Ladies and gentlemen, it's the "Alex Anderson Show."*
*The show about the world's most screwed up sixteen-year-old,*
*brought to you by . . . those wonderful folks, Bill and Clar-*
*ise. Tonight, see Alex fall apart on your local TV station.*
*Please stay tuned for the latest development.*

"Honey." Clarise gave me her big-eyed, sad-puppy look. "You
need to be there. It's important you go. You need closure. And you
owe it to Kevin and his family."

I don't owe anybody anything. Not now. Not ever. Who would
care if I was there? I was about to tell her off when Bill jumped in.

"Now, Alex." Bill said in his formal, I'm-the-father voice, the
one he uses when he wants to make a point. "Don't argue. Your
mother knows what's best. Besides, if you go, you'll feel better."

Good ol' Bill. He thinks he can solve every problem if he talks
like a sports announcer and sticks out his chest. He and Clarise
think they're the *cool* parents. Clarise is always reading the same nov-
els as Jenny, and Bill thinks that since he's memorized two songs by
Green Day he's in touch with the younger generation.

They don't know anything.

For all her tween books, age-inappropriate clothes, and insight
into teenagers, Clarise is all but useless. That may sound harsh, but
you don't live with her. She's always giving me this "get in touch
with your feelings" stuff and trying to tell me about how she "found
herself" when she traveled with some rock band an eon ago.

Whatever.

*I wish the two of them would just leave me alone.*

Right now, I could care less what either of them has to say.
Right now my life as I know it is over. It's dark and cold, and no
hovering adult is going to tell me what to do. I don't want to hear
how sorry they are, or how concerned they are, or how things will
get better soon . . . blah, blah, blah, blah. I just wish I could shut

them off, like I do the radio when a lame song comes on.

Right now, being dead doesn't sound like such a bad idea.


DID YOU EVER WANT to go back in time? I do. And I can tell you exactly how far back and where I would go: two weeks ago today, here in Stillwater, America.

Why?

Because that's when my best friend in the whole world died—some drunken scum driving a rusty pickup slammed into him and sprayed him all over the road.

That's why I'd go back.

I'd stop time for that one moment.

I'd stop time so Kevin wouldn't die.

# PART ONE

# CHAPTER ONE

OKAY SO THAT'S the story—Kev's dead. I'll tell you something else, too. I was there. Not that I want to talk about watching my best friend get his guts slammed all over the pavement, but my counselor, Therapy Chick, is making me write all this stuff down. We have this deal: I write about all the stuff that's bugging me, and she promises to keep Bill and Clarise from sending me away.

I've kept my end of the bargain—you're reading it—but you can bet I'll still end up getting screwed. Therapy Chick and Bill and Clarise will make sure of that. *But maybe, just maybe, if I keep writing . . .*

Since you already know Kevin is dead, you need to understand that his dying messed me up. See Kev and I grew up together. Most everybody assumes we've always been friends. Heck, some people think we're brothers.

Truth is, we were best friends.

Kev was the skinny, goofy-looking geek with the computer brain. I was the jock who protected him, the one who kept him from getting beat up at school. Our friendship began when I was three years old. Bill moved us to Stillwater (Bill's a professor of ancient music at Oklahoma State), and we settled into a big house on Countryside Drive. We hadn't lived there long when another family moved to the neighborhood—the Rubensteins.

The Rubensteins had two kids: a girl and a boy. The girl, Erin, was about seven. She always wore dresses and rode a pink bicycle; her teeth were locked in braces. She was a raging snot. I couldn't stand Erin at first, but her little brother was great.

He was my age with bright red hair. He drove a silver tricycle and he ate all the time. Didn't matter when or where or what time, Kevin was always munching on something. He liked to play, which is all that mattered, and he had the coolest stuff on the planet for us to play with, so long as you didn't try to make off with his favorite blanket or his stuffed gray cat.

His name was Kevin Gabriel Rubenstein, and we quickly forged a friendship. It didn't hurt that he was the only boy my age on the block—I sure wasn't playing trucks with his big sister—but I liked to think we would have been friends anyway.

Before long Kev (that's what I always called him) and I were inseparable. Clarise said we were "attached at the hip," but she was always smiling when she said it. She meant it in a good way. Even if she never understood the attraction.

By the time we hit kindergarten we were a known factor—no one bothered trying to get between us. I'm not sure what glue held us together, but I guess, well, we must have needed each other.

Kev was not the most athletic guy in the world. He was skinny, couldn't throw a baseball at all, and, yeah, he was the last guy picked for the team—no matter the sport. Being Jewish didn't help. The rednecks around here always called him names and made stupid jokes. It didn't help that he looked like a doofus. I mean a serious, USDA-Grade A doofus—a piece of string with feet.

Bill liked to say Kev was just skinny, that he'd fill out later.

"Kevin's fluid," he'd tell me. "He's built like a jet, aerodynamic."

"No," I'd said. "He's a pipe cleaner or a stick, plain and simple."

It didn't matter either way, because Kev was my friend. And what he lacked in muscle, he made up for in turbo-powered, rocket-scientist-quality brains.

*. . . Our special guest star tonight on the show, making an all too brief appearance is Kevin Rubenstein. Kevin will play the part of Alex's best friend.*

And me? Well, I played football, ran some track, and got in enough fights with the rest of the jocks that most of them left me alone. I guess that's why Kev and I hit it off so well. We each had our area in the friendship. I did the physical stuff, and Kev, well, Kev handled anything involving a book, a computer, or serious thinking.

KEV WAS ALSO A SHARER. He gave me chicken pox in first grade, mumps in second, and last year he loaned me some gross, stomach-thing that parked me in the bathroom for days. I remember spending most of my time puking. I was sleeping over at his house when my stomach blew for the first time.

"Sorry about infecting you with puker-ritus," Kev said with a laugh, as I raced for the bathroom.

Having paid homage to the toilet, I stumbled back downstairs, my gut cramping, like someone had it in a vice.

"It's okay. I just hurled on your bed," I told him.

The look on Kev's face was priceless as he raced past me to his room—and discovered I wasn't kidding.

So, yeah, you could say that, at times, our friendship bordered on weird. But that didn't detract from the fact that we'd become a two-headed, four-armed force that didn't take guff from anyone, that regularly outsmarted the A-listers at school, and that was known to be able to clean out a refrigerator in five seconds flat.

Of course, we did more than eat. We were behind all sorts of trouble and practical jokes, and we had a great time doing it all. And, honestly, our alliance constantly surprised people. The world looked at Kev and saw just a skinny geek, but there was so much more to him than that. He had a mind for mayhem. And a thing for art. Kev was the best artist I knew. He drew stuff all the time. It's what he wanted to do when he went to college.

"One of these days, you're going be watching my cartoons on TV," he told me one afternoon. "I have tons of ideas."

I believed him, too. He always carried a pencil and a sketchbook. He'd done it since third grade. That was when we were in Mrs. Talkington's class. She was this big lady who thought kids should sing, play, or draw. She never got mad and she always smiled. She also talked cool.

Kev thought she was the greatest teacher in the world, because she let him draw during his spare time in her class. When he finished a picture she'd post it on the bulletin board for everyone to admire.

"Master Kevin, you're going to be quite the artist someday," she would say. (Mrs. Talkington came from England and spoke with a formal, British accent.) "I *so* look forward to attending your first show."

"Thanks, mum," Kev always answered, with a smile.

Kev wasn't too concerned about conquering the art world; he just liked to draw. He was all about the pictures. I guess Mrs. Talkington must have figured that out, because by the time we made it out of third grade, he had covered most of her walls with them.

I still have one—a sketch of Kev and me standing in front of the Rubenstein Cartoon Studio.

I found it in his locker after he died.

# CHAPTER TWO

I T'S STRANGE. But it's getting harder and harder to remember all the fun things we once did together. All I can think about lately is weird, death-stuff. Somewhere in the back of my head all the fun memories have faded, like a picture left too long in the sun. Now, all I can remember is the day he died.

Most of the time I don't want to even think about Kev. But, it's like everything I do or everywhere I go, something happens to remind me my best friend is dead.

I'm sick of it.

The dreams won't go way, either. I fear closing my eyes for what I might see. I keep reliving that day, those last moments over and over again. I guess . . . I mean . . . now listen, I can't believe I'm writing this down *(and no, I haven't told my folks)* . . . maybe I can't get all of these images out of my head, because I'm . . . I'm the reason Kev died.

There, I said it.

I wrote it down.

Now you know.

I'm the reason Kevin is dead. I never told anybody what happened that day, I mean what *really* happened.

Until now.

THAT AFTERNOON WE SKIPPED sixth-hour art. We hardly ever skipped class. But that day, well, it was perfect. Late October, a Thursday. The school week was almost over. I'd just plopped into the seat next to Alicia Jennings *(a total babe)*, when I heard this strange hiss coming from the back of the room.

"Hey, Alexxx."

Kevin never could whisper very well—he always sounded like a boa constrictor with a lisp.

"What?"

"Let'ssss go, man."

"Huh? Go where? What are you talking about? We have art class."

"I know. I know. But I'm taking the resssst of the afternoon off."

Now, when El Brainiac wanted to skip art class, you took the request seriously. And he didn't need long to convince me. The weather was great: about fifty degrees with an ice-blue sky. All over town the maple and oak trees fought for attention.

I slipped out of class and joined him. Ten minutes later, we were cruising down the street. I gunned my Yamaha. The engine's roar filled my ears. My bike sounded deep and angry—as if it could chew you up and spit you out.

The Yamaha was new. The previous summer, Kev and I had gotten our motorcycle licenses. We'd saved for two years so both of us could buy new bikes once we were legal to ride. They were sweet, too. Mine was bright yellow with red trim. Kev's, jet black with a silver highlight.

We had sworn to our parents that we'd be careful on them, taken all kinds of driver safety classes, and bought (and promised to wear) helmets, but it was worth it. The Yamahas weren't top of the line, but they were much faster than Clarise liked, so I was happy.

That Thursday skipping school, I felt like I was sitting on a shiny, yellow rocket. We turned out of the back school parking lot. A few moments later we were on Washington Avenue and headed back to our side of town. We'd gone about a block, when Kev cut in front of me, turned, and slid sideways. I pulled up next to him and put on the brake. Kev's helmet was off, and he had a weird look on his face.

"So, ya' still mad?"

I'd been mad since some guys at school that morning had teased me about being a virgin. Kev had joined in, and, for a while, it had left me pretty riled. Later, Kev made a point of telling me that he had just been kidding, but I was still frosted at him.

I'd stopped and pushed my visor up. "Huh?"

Kev mouthed the words again, like I couldn't hear.

"Are . . . you . . . still . . . pissssed . . . off?"

"Nooo," I yelled back. "Not too much. I just figured you'll always be a turd. I'm used to it."

Okay, I lied. But it was no big deal; we never stayed mad at each other for too long. Kev must have sensed I wasn't coming completely clean with him, because he kept talking and waving his arms, trying to apologize, I guess. Jeez, he looked like a dancing praying mantis.

"Don't fall all over yourself being nice or anything." Kev rolled his eyes in exasperation.

I leaned toward him and yanked my helmet off.

"Listen dork, you've been a moron all day, and I've been pretty cool about it. So don't push your luck, okay?"

Kev was quiet for a long time. Instead of saying anything, he started panting. I thought he was going to hack up a lung or something. Then he started to cough. After he finished spewing snot everywhere, I asked him what was wrong.

"Nothing," he said.

"So why are you being such a jerk?"

Kev smiled, sheepishly. "Look, I'm sorry, okay? I didn't mean to tick you off. I was just joking about the virgin stuff."

I smiled. I wasn't mad any longer.

"So what's bugging you?"

Kev kicked a stick with his shoe.

"Do . . . do you remember that girl I told you about?"

"Which one?"

"The tall one with the killer green eyes and the big . . . "

"Oh yeah. What's her name?"

"Darla."

I wrapped my arms around my chest, until my fingers were tickling my back, and started pursing my lips, like I was sucking on some girl's face. "Yeah, Dar-link. Oh my Dar-link! I love you, Dar-link."

"No, funny man! Dar-la! Could you be serious just for once?"

"Chill, Kev!" I laughed. "I was teasing! So, yeah, I remember her. Aren't you supposed to take her to the homecoming dance?"

"Haven't asked her yet."

"What? Have you forgot? The dance is next Friday."

"I know, but I'm . . . I'm not sure she'll go."

I pointed back over my shoulder towards the school.

"And you say I'm a moron. Jeez, Kev, you'll never know unless you ask. Idiot! The worst she can do is tell you 'no.' "

"But what if she says 'no' because I'm . . ."

"Because you're what?"

"You know, because . . . I'm Jewish."

I rolled my eyes.

"What a dolt! You have to be the biggest idiot in the tenth grade. Who cares? You're a great guy. Heck, you could make a dead guy laugh. Who gives a flip if you're Jewish? Paint one of those Star-of-Ralph symbols on your chest and tell her you're an ace crime fighter."

Kev snorted, then laughed—a loud obnoxious, through-his-nose, hissing, wheezing laugh.

"It's Star of David, you idiot," he said. "S-t-a-r o-f D-a-v-i-d."

Then his smile faded.

"I don't know Alex. You don't get it. The other kids aren't like you. They call me 'Jew-boy' or 'Kike.' Even the girls do it sometimes."

Kev's face had turned bright red.

"Then there's the ever popular 'Christ-killer.' " He stared down at the pavement. "That one's my favorite."

We had been down this road before. Back when we were both in sixth grade, a bunch of Stillwater's more popular idiots decided they were going to spend the school year messing with Kev, because he was a Jew. It took several thrashings by yours truly before they let it go. And though Kev never said anything, I could tell it messed with his head. We talked more than once that year about how to deal with bigots. Then we got back to doing what we loved: eating pizza and watching zombie movies.

Everything had been cool in the bigot department for a long time, so I figured somebody (probably Darla's ex-boyfriend, Scott Williams) must have said something. I knew being teased bugged Kev, but I wanted him to know everything would be okay.

"Look, just ignore it, okay?" I whacked him upside the head. "Darla doesn't care if you're Jewish. She just wants to know that you don't smell bad and that you have enough cash to pay for food. So ask her, okay? Trust me. I know about this stuff."

"Okay. Okay, I will. I'll call her tonight."

"Good. Now since I solved your girl problem. You get to help me solve mine."

"What's that?"

"A Coke. I'm thirsty and you're buying!"

# CHAPTER THREE

I GRABBED MY HELMET, flipped the visor down, twisted the gas, and took off. I wanted to make it to the end of Oak Street before Kev caught up. I could feel him on my tail. We roared down Oak then crossed Cyprus, over to Elm. Kev weaved in and out of the cars parked along the street. I slowed, up shifted, hit the throttle, and slipped past him.

Elm Street was a great place to ride. It's about fifteen blocks long and lined with a million tall trees. The dogs that live along it are fat, old, and slow. The lawns are hilly and smooth.

Kev and I were now neck and neck. Zipping through the small circle drive at the Larson house, I managed to pass him. Kev saw me go, turned, and shifted into third. I gritted my teeth and jumped the curb at Elm and Fourth.

Kev swerved, pulled in front of me, hit the throttle, and screamed, "Move it, douche bag!"

The Patented Wildman Motorcycle Race had begun. The wildman motorcycle race usually took place on a long stretch of University Drive, but today we were all over the place. To win the race, you had to ride wide open until the other driver either ran out of gas, got stopped by the cops, or chickened out.

The fact is *(man, I hate to admit this even now)* Kev usually beat me, a fact I found surprising.

But today felt different. Today it was too close to call. As we turned onto Division, neither of us gave an inch. My bike screamed through the chilly, fall air. It took all my skill to keep up with Kev and not lose control. Kev zigzagged in front of me and flipped me off. He was pretty good with the drive-like-a-moron-cut-off-your-best-friend move.

You gotta understand about racing with Kev. The rules were simple: There were no rules. It was every man for himself and Kev did not like to lose. I know, you'd think that since he wasn't any bigger than a pencil, he'd be easy to beat. But there was something about him on a motorcycle that made him, well, it made him dangerous. I swear, he could think quicker and drive faster than anybody I ever knew. He had no fear. He was awesome.

Nine out of ten times, he'd win.

But not this time. This time I was winning. This time he was mine. Or so I thought. I'd just cranked it through the intersection of University and Seventh, when ol' Mrs. Gore pulled her boat-sized Cadillac out and blocked the street. Kev managed to get around her.

I wasn't so lucky.

I gunned my bike, went right, dodged a row of mailboxes, and opened it back up. I was still within a few yards of Kev. He turned and flipped me off for about the billionth time. I had the throttle wide open by then. My tachometer redlined.

Then, suddenly, Kev slowed. I got him, I thought. I sailed past him. I was almost to Red Plains Avenue when I realized he wasn't behind me or beside me or in front of me. I looked in my mirror; there he was, about a block back. I pulled over, stopped, and waited.

And waited.

And waited.

I figured he had engine trouble, so I finally turned and drove back to where I'd last seen him. When I got there, I got off my bike to see if he needed help. Kev waited until I was standing next to him, then opened his bike up and roared past me, screaming at the top of his lungs: "Sucker!"

I jumped back on my bike and raced after him, feeling the rush of air and the throb of the motor as I downshifted to avoid a slowly moving cat. Kev was still about a hundred yards ahead of me. We were almost to Red Plains. This time I was going to take him. Seriously, I was tired of losing. I leaned forward, pushed the throttle to max, and slipped in front of him, just before Red Plains Parkway. Hall of Fame Avenue was the next intersection, and I was pretty sure I was far enough ahead that I'd win if I rode wide open.

I was wrong.

I had to back off the throttle and pull to the side to avoid some guy in a Toyota who appeared out of nowhere. Kev went through two driveways, jumped the curb, and cut in front of me.

I remember screaming every four-letter word I knew. Then, as if to make sure that I knew he was still the king, Kev stomped on the gas, looked at me, and gave me the ol' one-finger salute—again.

He shouldn't have.

Because while he was looking at me, Kev didn't see the stoplight at Division and Hall of Fame change to red. Usually, it would have been fine; it's not that busy of a street.

Not today.

A few months ago the city council okayed construction to begin on the Perkins Bypass. And today, because of all that construction, some guy who had had a few too many drinks took Hall of Fame home to avoid the cops. It was like watching a scene in a movie gone horribly wrong. I could feel myself silently screaming, "Stop!"—but no sound came out.

Kev was moving forward on his bike, but he had his head turned towards me. He was acting stupid. From the right, out of the corner of my eye, I saw the yellow-and-white, beat-up pickup. The truck was weaving in and out of traffic; its driver obviously not paying attention to whether the lights were red or green. I watched Kev start to turn away, but he was too slow to see what was headed for him. I tried to yell again, but the words didn't come quickly enough.

He was in the center of the intersection when the truck hit him—broadside. There was no screeching or tires squealing or anything like that. There was just a sickening thud and then the piercing, grating sound of Kev's bike breaking in half and sliding down the street. Sparks flew everywhere. The impact hit Kev so hard that he sailed up into the air, fell face down on the pavement, then flipped over and over and over across the street, like a mangled toy doll tossed from a car window.

The truck kept going—grinding and scraping and dragging pieces of Kev's bike underneath it. Eventually the driver skidded into a lamppost and stopped.

Behind him, a hundred yards or so back, Kev lay face down on the pavement. He had his helmet on but underneath him a pool of blood was forming.


THE REST IS BURNED INTO my brain: People screaming, police sirens wailing—and shards of motorcycle scattered up and down the street. Cops everywhere. The smell of gasoline in the air. The ambulance arriving. The flurry of paramedics.

Everything was slow motion. I just stood there, numb, watching like I was at the drive-in, as the ambulance turned on its flashing red lights and pulled away with my best friend inside.

Somehow *(and to this day I can't tell you how)* I remembered my cell phone and called home. Bill was out of town, so I got Clarise.

"There's . . . there's been . . .! Kev's been hit . . . hurry!"

My hands shook so hard I could barely hold the phone.

"Alex, honey? What's wrong? Where are you?"

"Hurry, there's been an accident Clarise—meet me at the emergency room!"

It took me ten more minutes to explain what had happened, but

I finally got through to her.  Then just as I was getting on my bike, the cops cornered me with a billion questions.  I'd probably still be there trying to give them answers, but some lady in a blue Dodge pulled over, flung open her door, and started running towards me, yelling and waving her hands.  While the cops were distracted by her, I slipped away, jumped back on my bike, and raced to the hospital.

The sun was an orange fireball, and the sky was tinged red, purple, and pink.  I remember thinking Kev would like those colors —he used them a lot in his art.  It seemed strange to be riding so fast without him.  I made it to the emergency room in record time. I stomped on the brake, dropped my bike, and bolted through the door.  I ran down the hall, yelling for Kev.

I didn't get far.

A doctor stopped me.  He was tall with silver-white hair and a starched lab coat.  He looked like one of the professors who worked with Bill at the university.

"Excuse me.  Can I help you?"

I pointed towards the main hallway.

"My . . . best . . . my best friend was in a motorcycle accident; they brought him here.  I want to see if he's okay."

Jerk Doctor moved in front of me.

"Why don't you wait back here?" he said.  "Someone will be with you shortly."

Jerk Doctor then grabbed me by the arm and pulled me towards the front door of the emergency room.

"But I, I just wanted . . ."

It was obvious I wasn't getting past the guy.  Jerk Doctor stood in front of me for a few more minutes, rattling on about hospital policy.  Then his beeper went off.

"You'll have to excuse me," he said.  "Why you don't call back later?  Perhaps someone could help you then."

He pushed me through the doors and outside.  I walked over and sat down on a bench near the entrance.  The Jerk Doctor dashed back into the ER and disappeared.  I must have kicked about a million rocks trying to figure out what to do next, when a plump, gray-headed nurse walked past me headed for the building.

I stood and walked towards her.

"Hey, could you help me?"

"I'll try, son. What's the problem?"

"Well my best—my brother—was just in an accident, and our mom isn't here yet. I'm scared, and I was wondering if you could tell me . . . "

At first, I wasn't sure if she'd bought my lie or not. Then she put her arm around my shoulder and walked me back inside the emergency room.

"You wait right here, and I'll see what I can find out."

"Thanks," I said.

I plopped down on a bench and began the rest of the worst day of my life.


IT WASN'T LONG BEFORE Clarise and Jenny arrived. I watched them hurdle chairs and sling clipboards out of the way to get to me. Clarise skidded to a stop where I was sitting.

"Oh Alex, honey, honey are you okay?" she asked, as she ran her fingers through my hair. "Oh gosh, what happened? Where's Kevin?"

I pointed to a glassed-in area with drawn curtains.

"I think he's pretty screwed up. They won't let me see him."

Jenny just sat there, numb, a vacant look on her face.

The plump nurse returned with news. It wasn't good.

"I'm sorry, but unless you're immediate family, I am not at liberty to discuss your friend's condition. Is there someone I can call for you?"

Clarise grabbed my hand.

"We need to find a doctor," she told the nurse.

I watched her go from person to person, looking for somebody official. She disappeared down a hall. A few minutes later, she came back with Jerk Doctor, the same moron who didn't want me in the ER in the first place.

"Doctor, how's Kev?"

Jerk Doctor stood there, twisting his stethoscope.

"Pardon me, are you a family member?" he asked.

"Aw, well, like I said before, I'm . . . see . . . Kev's my best . . ."

Clarise interrupted.

"He's Kevin's brother." She pointed to Jenny. "And this is his sister. I'm Kevin's aunt. Now will you please tell us the extent of my nephew's injuries?"

"I'm sorry, ma'am, but I should talk to the boy's parents first. Excuse me."

Jerk Doctor turned and walked back through the double glass doors. The plump nurse gave me a sad look, grabbed a tray full of medical supplies, and followed the doctor.

Clarise touched my arm.

"I'm sorry, honey. I guess we'll just have to wait."

She didn't say much after that. None of us did. We just sat and stared at the wall, for fear of what we might see in each other's eyes.

"I was there."

I didn't finish the sentence. Clarise reached for me. Her hands soft and warm. For the first time since I was five years old, I didn't pull away. Jenny laid her head on my shoulder.

More doctors came and went, racing back and forth. For a while, it was nonstop action. Then the doctors and some lab people started to drift back down the hall. They all looked serious and sad. Nobody said anything. They just shook their heads and walked past us as if we were part of the furniture.

I grabbed a skinny lab-guy by his white coat.

"Hey! Can't you tell me what's going on? How's Kev?"

"I'm sorry, but no," he said. "Someone will come to speak with you in a minute."

Skinny Guy darted back behind a screen. So Clarise, Jenny, and I continued our vigil. Every now and again, I heard the squish of some nurse's shoes on the tile floor. I would look up, hoping for news, but nobody came. Above us, the fluorescent lights in the ceiling buzzed. Clarise sat next to me, holding a wrinkled, coffee-stained copy of the Stillwater NewsPress. She wasn't reading it.

"Alex, honey, maybe we should . . . "

I was just about to cut her off when someone called my name.

"Alex? Clarise?"

Kev's mom raced down the hall towards us. She must have run every red light in three counties getting to the hospital. She worked in Tulsa, and it was at least an hour and a half away. She looked frazzled and strange—she'd been crying, and her face was all blotchy and red. I watched her jog to the emergency room admitting window, shouting questions about Kev to the attendant.

The plump nurse took her by the arm, and they walked to a room at the end of hall. The door stayed shut for a few minutes, then Mrs. Rubenstein came out. She swayed toward the three of us in slow motion.

"Alex . . ."

She drifted past Clarise. She placed her hands on my shoulders. Makeup streaked her face. Her eyes were red, and she was breathing fast, as if she'd just run five miles.

"Alex, there was . . . "

She took a deep breath. Huge tears rolled down her face.

"His injuries were too severe. His brain stopped."

"Oh, no!" My head whirled. "What was going on? No! No! No! We were just racing. I never meant . . . "

"Alex, Kevin is . . . "

She couldn't bring herself to say it. But I knew.

Kevin was dead.

The way the doctors and the plump nurse had avoided talking to us. It was all so clear. Kev was dead.

What were we to do now? Mrs. Rubenstein wouldn't let me go. She smelled of hair spray, sweat, and perfume. I felt sick. I'd just watched Kev die. I wanted to puke. Instead we stood there with our arms around each other sobbing. It was like we were doing some strange dance. After a few moments, she let go and stepped back. She swayed for a second, then fell to the floor.

I swear if I live to be a thousand years old I'll never forget those next few minutes, because Kev's mom proceeded to come completely unglued. She sat on the floor, sobbing and crying out. And over and over again, she asked the same question: "Why? Why? Why?"

She rocked back and forth, begging for an answer that would never come. Clarise hurried to comfort her, and Jenny followed. Together, they lifted Mrs. Rubenstein onto a hospital bench in the waiting room. Clarise held her like a baby.

"Not my little boy!" She whimpered. "Not my little boy! Why? Why? Why?"

Just when it seemed it couldn't get any worse, Kev's dad arrived. He saw me. He saw Clarise and Jenny trying to calm his wife, and it didn't take him long to figure things out. He bolted down the hall, shouting, "Kevin? Son?"

Jerk Doctor stopped him, and five minutes later, Kev's dad stumbled back down the hall to the waiting room, like a drunken, pale ghost. He walked straight to me. His face twisted into a red, tense knot. He grabbed me and lifted me off the floor. I thought he was going to break my spine.

"My son is gone!" He said it over and over. "He's gone!"

He started to cry and his face turned angry and dark. He held me out at arms length and looked me in the eyes.

"You killed him!" he screamed. "The doctor said he was hit early this afternoon. What in the hell were you two doing out of school? What were you doing racing those damn motorcycles?"

"I . . . we . . . Kev wanted . . . " I tried to answer him, but the words wouldn't come.

Clarise tried to force her way between us, yelling at Mr. Rubenstein to let me go. Jenny pulled on his arms, trying to release me. Mr. Rubenstein jerked himself away from Jenny and pushed me up against the wall.

"My son would be alive if he hadn't gone with you! You knew better. You killed him! You stupid little . . ."

I went limp and slipped out of his arms. Then I puked all over him and the floor.

"What is wrong with you?" he shouted.

I left him trying to clean my puke off his slacks, as I stumbled out of the emergency room into the night air. I fell into the grass. My guts churned, like a million snakes were crawling inside me. I felt both numb and sick to my stomach. I puked again. This time, all over myself. Above me the sky swelled a deep purple.

A lightning bolt split the dark.

I'd killed my best friend.

In my head, I could still hear Mrs. Rubenstein's cries and Mr. Rubenstein's screams. I'd killed their son. I'd killed Kevin. I rolled over and puked again. The snakes in my gut writhed.

Then the rain began.

# CHAPTER FOUR

THINGS DID NOT IMPROVE over the weekend. By the time the Tulsa television stations finished replaying the story, the whole world had watched another kid die too young. I'll never forget the footage of them loading Kev's body in the ambulance. Of course, the newspapers played it up big, too. Most of them splashed a bloody picture of the accident scene—combined with shots of Kev and me from last year's yearbook and the story—across their front page.

Above the fold, of course.

The headlines were the worst: "Questions Remain About Student's Motorcycle Death," one screamed. Another reminded everyone: "Accident Still Being Investigated." My favorite was the headline on the first story that broke after the wreck: "Youth's Life Cut Short in Tragic Motorcycle Accident."

At home, the phone wouldn't quit ringing. I got sick of talking to detectives and the idiots at the medical examiner's office. Then there were the calls from the school counselor, the minister at the church where Bill and Clarise go, and all of Jenny's little friends.

"Is it true?" I overheard one girl ask Jenny. "Did Alex see him die? I mean, he was there—why didn't he stop him?"

School was worse.

And, just so you know, I now hated everyone there.

After the accident, I couldn't go anywhere at Stillwater High without people staring or whispering. At first, it was like no one dared say anything to me, but then every time I walked down the hall or into a class, I heard the whispers.

> . . . It's the "Insensitive Idiot Hour" on the After School Special. Today, you'll learn just how stupid and idiotic your classmates can be. Especially when someone dies . . .

A few kids stopped me in the hall to tell me how sorry they were, but I could tell it was bull. No sooner would they walk off, then I'd hear them whispering to each other about how I had been at the accident, how I had been the one who saw it, and how I hadn't done anything to keep Kev alive.

I was being eaten alive.

About a week later, Mrs. Howerton, the principal, caught me in the parking lot. I figured she was going to rag on me, too. But she didn't. She just looked at me and said she wanted to talk. I ditched my bike and walked back inside school with her.

Mrs. Howerton reminds me of my grandmother—she's tall, kind of stringy and long, with hair frozen from too much hair spray. She smelled like old lady perfume, all sweet and musty at the same time. But I guess for a principal, she's probably no worse than any other. She wasn't one to yell or scream at students, but she's also not afraid to get in your face when you tick her off.

Today, she was trying to be nice—too nice. It made me nervous. We walked down the hall toward the Junior Section. The school was deserted, almost tomb-like. Mrs. Howerton stopped at the office and grabbed two cardboard boxes. She took one and handed me the other. It took me a second to realize our destination was Kev's locker. Neither of us said anything. We walked to the middle of the hall. She stopped and looked at me, then sat her box on the floor.

"Alex, I tried contacting Kevin's parents, but I haven't been able to reach them. So, I thought you might want to help me."

Another long pause.

"I thought you'd want to be here to help clean out Kevin's locker. You don't have to, only if you feel like it."

Cleaning out Kev's stuff was about the last thing I wanted to do, but I didn't want his stuff to get trashed, either. I guess I also needed something of his. Something that proved we were friends. So instead of walking off, which I think is what Mrs. Howerton kind of expected me to do, I stood there, holding the empty box, a stupid look on my face.

Mrs. Howerton found Kev's locker. She spun the dial and opened the metal door. Inside it looked like a tiny art studio. Funny, in all the time I'd known Kev, I had never looked inside.

On the walls were this drawing of Kev and me on our bikes as well as a bunch of other pictures. Kev had tacked up a photo of Darla, the girl he wanted to ask to the dance. His books were all stacked neatly in the center underneath a drawing of a superhero he called Ralph. Ralph had a big Star of David on his chest and wore a long yellow cape (*a big inside joke between Kev and me*).

Mrs. Howerton pulled out Kev's papers, textbooks, and other leftover stuff. At first I thought she was going to toss them, but instead she smiled and handed them to me.

"I understand how upset you are. I thought there might be something you'd like to keep."

She was trying to be kind, but it didn't help. She took Kev's chemistry and English books and stacked them on the floor. Then she grabbed his battered biology textbook.

I sniffled a couple of times and wiped my eyes on my sleeve.

"Alex?" She stacked the biology book on top of the others. "Are you sure you're okay? We can do this later, if you'd prefer."

I didn't say anything. I just grabbed Kev's papers and notebooks and stuffed them in the box, while Mrs. Howerton took a good look to make sure we hadn't missed anything.

"Oh, Alex, here's one more."

Mrs. Howerton handed me a thin, orange binder. On the cover Kev had sketched the image of a box in the shape of a human heart wrapped with a bow. Below it he'd written, "Organ Donors . . . Giving the Ultimate Gift."

"Guess he did finish it."

"Finished what?" Mrs. Howerton said.

I stopped.

I didn't realize I had spoken out loud.

"Uh, this." I pointed to the orange notebook. "Kev was working on a report about organ donation for Mr. Anderson's current events class. He spent a whole bunch of time on it."

Mrs. Howerton cocked her head.

"That's an interesting subject for a boy from a Jewish family."

"Yeah, that's what his folks said, too. Kev said some Jews don't believe in donating their organs—they call it 'desecration of the body.' He and his folks had some serious talks about it, but in the end, he convinced them. He even wrote this rabbi in New York. The rabbi wrote him back, encouraging him and everything."

Whew. It was the most I had spoken in weeks. I didn't know why I was telling Mrs. Howerton about Kev's project, but it seemed like she wanted to listen. I looked at my feet. Images of Kev sprawled and lifeless on the street filled my head.

"He was pretty serious about it. He said he wanted to be . . . "

Tears rolled down my face.

"Alex, are you okay?"

Mrs. Howerton moved towards me. I stepped away from her. I mean, that's all I needed, right? To cry in front of the principal? I felt like a total moron.

". . . an organ donor."

Mrs. Howerton didn't say anything more, but I saw her dab at her eyes with a tissue. She grabbed a few more stray papers from

Kevin's locker, and we were done. Locker 521 was empty, like no one had ever used it.

I grabbed the box with Kev's stuff and ran to my bike.

I TOOK THE LONG way home. It was almost five when I turned into our driveway. The trees looked all spiky and weird against the deep red sunset. Clarise met me at the door.

"Honey, Alex, are you okay?"

I pushed my way past her and headed up the stairs to my room.

"Alex?"

"I'm fine. Okay?"

Clarise stood at the bottom of the staircase. She looked like she wasn't sure whether to be mad or sad.

"Well, if you need to talk I'm here? Okay?"

*No thanks, Clarise. I've done my talking for the day.*

> *. . . We now continue our regular broadcast of "The Screwed-Up Life of Alex Anderson."*

THE NEXT DAY I WAS LATE for school. At that point, I didn't care what happened to me, and I certainly didn't care about who started World War I, so I skipped history, cruised through Sonic, and grabbed a large coffee. By the time I made it back to campus, the second-hour bell was ringing. I slipped into biology class and grabbed a seat about five rows from the back. It didn't take me long to realize that I should have stayed at Sonic.

Two rows behind me Tiffany Synder leaned towards her friend, Kaylee Something-or-the-Other. Tiffany then pointed at me and whispered under her breath.

"Yeah, that's him. Everyone says he saw Kevin die. They were racing or something."

Kaylee gave her a wide-eyed "I didn't know that" look.

"Why were they racing? Did Alex try to help Kevin? How come Alex didn't get hurt?"

"I don't know, but that's what everyone's been asking?" Tiffany whispered. "I hear the police say he's still a suspect. Negligent homicide or something, I think."

I took a long slug of my coffee. Anger boiled inside me. It was amazing. Everyone was suddenly an expert on Kev's death. It was all such a lie. I slammed my book shut. I didn't want to sit in class anymore. I wasn't going to listen to some girls—neither of whom knew Kev—act as if they were heartbroken by his death. Hell, in all the time Kev had gone to this school, Tiffany had never once spoken a word to him. She didn't even know his last name.

I grabbed my book, stood, and headed for the door.

I should have stayed in my seat.

As I reached the door, I heard the low voice of Scott Williams.

"Good job, Anderson," he hissed. "You got rid of the Jew; now if you can take out those spicks in fourth hour, this school might just become respectable again."

At his words, my sadness and anger and rage exploded in my gut. It was like my belly was busting with angry snakes. I whirled around, grabbed my chair, and hurled it straight at Scott. It caught him right in the face. I saw the blood and I heard the bones snap.

"Screw you Scott! Screw all of you!"

I threw my textbook at the back wall and pointed at Tiffany.

"Were you there?" I screamed. "Did you see Kev die? He was my best friend, and all you and your friends have done is gossip and lie about the accident. You don't know anything. I hate all of you!"

I kicked the door of the classroom open and ran down the hall.

A few minutes later the police arrived.


THAT FRIDAY MRS. HOWERTON came to see Bill and Clarise at our house. The three of them sat in our living room and talked for a long time. I was exiled to the kitchen. I tried to listen, but they were huddled together and they talked quietly, so I couldn't overhear much of what they were saying. Every now and then I'd catch a snatch of conversation:

". . . not appropriate behavior for a boy of his skill and intelligence," Mrs. Howerton said.

Bill mumbled in agreement.

". . . still upset over the death of Kevin."

Clarise seemed to agree.

". . . perhaps some counseling or treatment. We're all very concerned about Alex."

Yeah right. Other than my little trip to Kev's locker, nobody at school had acted as if they cared about how Kev's death had hit me.

Later that night my parents gave me the bad news: I'd been suspended from school for the rest of the semester, and it was "recommended" that I seek mental health treatment. If I wanted to return to school it was required. Bill tried to play it off as no big deal.

"Alex, we'll find you a good counselor. They can help. They really can. It's nothing to be ashamed about. You just need someone to talk to about the accident."

Wrong. What I needed was to get out of this stupid town. I need to be gone—somewhere, anywhere, it didn't matter where. I just wanted to disappear. I crawled into the bed and turned off the light. It felt like the world was ending, and I was the guy who had pushed the start button.

Did it get any worse?

That would be yes.

# CHAPTER FIVE

S INCE I HAD TO stay home from school, Bill and Clarise made sure I had a list of things to do each day. The list was long, mostly housekeeping chores—vacuum the den or empty the trash. On this particular Tuesday, however, I was supposed to rake the leaves in the front yard and clean off the pool cover. Nothing too difficult, and, honestly, I didn't mind, at least it was something to do.

I'd just finished hosing off the pool cover when my cell phone buzzed. Last year, because I'd pulled an "A" in music appreciation, Bill had bought me this sweet iPhone. I loved the texting and the streaming video, but my favorite feature was the seven-bazillion ringtones he had added before he gave it to me.

Some of them were dumb. I mean some of the music was Bill's. But a bunch of the tones were from songs I liked, as well as some cool older stuff that Bill had downloaded for me.

Anyway that Tuesday, as I sat down in a deck chair to take a break, Jimi Hendrix's "All Along the Watchtower" started playing—that was my general "somebody wants to talk to me" ring. I pulled the phone out of my pocket and tapped the glass.

"Yeah, this is Alex."

"Alex, Coach Knott."

"Hey coach. What's up?"

"Alex, son, we need to talk. We have . . . "

I knew he was going to say "a problem" before he said it.

"You're a great kid with a bright future." Coach's voice was shaky and he sounded weird. "And I love having ya on the team. But this little incident the other day in biology has, ahhh, well, the secondary activities association won't let you, and, well, Mrs. Howerton thinks, and I don't like it either, but . . ."

Coach Knott wasn't much of a talker. Usually he was more of a yeller. At practice, he barked orders and cussed you out if you didn't run the play right. Today's conversation was requiring more communication skills than he had in his toolkit.

"Coach, what's going on?"

Coach Knott stopped talking. I could hear him breathing in and out, like he was forcing himself to stay calm.

"Son, now that you've been suspended I can't let you play football. The rules don't allow it, and if we tried to play you, we'd have to forfeit the game."

"But I thought?"

"I'm sorry Alex."

"How long?"

Coach Knott paused.

"Huh?" he said.

"I asked, how long. How long am I off the team? I'm only suspended from school for the rest of the semester."

"I know that Alex," Coach said, "but I gotta think of the other players. Like I said, you're a great player. But, well, the other boys, they voted and . . . "

"So I'm kicked off the team for good?"

More breathing on the other end of the phone line.

"Yeah, Alex, I'm sorry. I sure hate this, especially after your friend died and all. But, well son, there's no other way. Now, if you want to, when you're a senior we could try . . ."

It took me two years worth of hard work, summer weight training, and a million mornings of running before dawn to make the team. Now, with one phone call, it was over.

I hung up before he could finish his sentence.

> *. . . We regret to inform you that the "Alex Anderson Sports Spectacular," normally broadcast on this station, has been canceled for the immediate future. Please stay tuned for different programming.*

THINGS WENT DOWNHILL quickly after that. After I was kicked off the team, it seemed like the rest of the world turned dark. Football was a big deal. I'd worked hard and earned a starting tailback position. When other things in my life went wrong, football was something that, well, that helped me stay focused.

But like Kev's life, football was over, too.

Since I wouldn't be allowed to play for the rest of the year, as far as I could see, I had no reason to care about going back to school. I did my time at home, lived in sweats most days, and slept late.

Twice a week I met with Therapy Chick.

Therapy Chick was supposed to be my counselor, my grief counselor I guess you'd call her. I don't know how much Bill and Clarise paid her, but whatever it was, it was too much, because Therapy Chick was useless. As far as I could tell, she was more interested in what I was wearing or who was calling her or what part of her makeup needed retouching, than she was in helping me get over Kev's death. Once in a while, she'd write something down or plop her face in her hands and lean in close to me, like she was trying to figure me out.

Most of time, though, I just sat in her office and answered her stupid questions.

"Are you still having the dreams?"

"Yeah."

"Are they still about Kevin's death?"

"Yeah."

"Is it the same dream?"

"Yeah."

"Can you describe it?"

"No."

"Alex, you have to help me help you."

"I've told you all this before." It was never an interesting ex-change. Usually I left feeling worse than when I came in. That didn't seem to bother Bill and Clarise. They made me go every Tuesday and Thursday. This Tuesday, the session had gone particularly poor-ly. Therapy Chick kept telling me I had to learn to express myself.

"Alex, I can't help you if you won't open up," she said.

I rolled my eyes. "There's not a whole lot to say. You know the story. You know why I was kicked out of school. What else do you want to hear?"

Therapy Chick did her lean-in-thing again.

"I want to hear how you feel."

"Yeah, right."

She pushed herself back in her chair, grabbed a pen, and started writing. I sat there, listening for the clock to chime so I could leave. Therapy Chick continued to write.

"If you're too busy, I could leave early," I offered.

More writing.

"I mean, wouldn't that help you get ready for your next client?"

"Hang on," she said, continuing to scribble. "Just a sec."

I turned and looked out the window. The clock chimed. Finally, I was free. I got up to leave just as Therapy Chick put down her pen. She handed me an envelope.

"Please see that your parents get this." She gave me a look that said I'd better not forget. "And, Alex?"

"Yeah?"

"You'll need to have them call the number on the inside within twenty-four hours or I will contact your parents myself. Understood?"

Suddenly I didn't feel so good.


"I JUST DON'T UNDERSTAND. Alex seems more and more depressed. Yet it's been more than six months since Kevin's death."

Bill was on the phone to Therapy Chick—for the third time this week. I grabbed my bedroom phone and slipped into my closet and shut the door. I scrunched down underneath the shelf and pressed the phone close to my ear. Yeah, I was listening in on the extension. I figured this was my life, and it only seemed fair that I know what everyone else was trying to do with it. As I listened, Bill kept going on and on, telling her how concerned he was and how I wasn't acting like myself. *Why couldn't I have been an orphan?*

Therapy Chick kept pushing for what she called "intense counseling"—sessions three or four times a week combined with "an open, honest dialogue" between Bill, Clarise, and me. Bill kept saying, "Oh my" and "Do you think all that's necessary?"

Then they hung up. A little while later, I heard Bill call her back. I slipped into the closet and picked up the extension—nothing, only the hum of an unused phone line. Rats! He'd caught me. This time he'd called from his cell phone. If he wanted it that way, it was fine by me. But if Bill and Therapy Chick wanted to know what to do, the answer was simple: leave me alone.


IT'S QUIET, ABOUT THREE in the morning. Bill and Clarise were asleep—I could hear their snores all the way down to my room. Bill sounded like a chainsaw.

It was cold outside. Winter had hit Oklahoma hard, with lots of ice and snow. Christmas was over, and the new semester had started. I was back in class—when I felt like going. It's been forever since Kev died, but the dreams won't go away. Every night the same nightmare played, as if on a loop: I relive Kev dying in slow motion. I see the crash over and over. Then I look at my hands covered in blood.

The thoughts have been in my head for a while now. Dark and ugly, they haunt me as relentlessly as the images of the accident. I want out. I want it to be over—the end.

I want to be dead.

There, I said it.

The other day I was playing around on the Internet, and I found this guy's website. It showed how he'd planned his own suicide. He kept a daily diary of how he felt, then on the last entry, he simply said good-bye.

That's where I am. I don't want to be messed up anymore.

I just want to go to sleep . . . forever.

I CLIMBED OUT OF BED and walked to my closet. Inside the closet is a sack. Inside the sack is the way to solve my problem: Bill's revolver. I found it the other day in the garage. Bill collects all sorts of stuff and not long ago he bought a box of odds and ends at an estate sale. Inside the box was the revolver—a .38-caliber—and some bullets. The gun was new, never been fired.

Bill said he didn't want it in the house. Clarise thought he threw it away, but Bill never throws anything away. Instead, he stashed it on a shelf in the garage and forgot about it. I had found it putting up the Christmas lights.

I slipped the .38 into my sweats. I brought the bullets in from the garage a few days later. Now I had a way to end the pain. A quick, easy way to finish it—one shot and everything would be over. Then peace. No more pain. No more nightmares. No more guilt. No more whispers. Just sleep.

I crawled inside the closet, shut the door, and reached up and behind the books on the top shelf, next to my old computer games.

The paper crinkled as I pulled the sack to my lap and felt for the gun inside. It would never occur to Bill that I might take his gun. But I have. A few days ago I loaded it. Five rounds in all. I touched the barrel—it was smooth and cool.

I pulled back the hammer and pushed the gun against my forehead. My finger touched the trigger.

No, not now.

I put the gun back in the sack. Before I can go for good, I needed to do a few things first—like that guy on the Internet. I need to write some stuff down and make a plan. Then, when everyone is gone and the house is empty, I can check out.

I put the sack back on the shelf. The darkness returned. I'm not yet asleep, but the dream has returned anyway. With sweat rolling down my neck, here in the dark, I relive the past.

A COUPLE OF WEEKS AGO I saw Kev's sister Erin at the grocery store. She was getting in her car when she saw me coming out the door. She started towards me across the parking lot, like she wanted to talk.

I didn't.

I turned and ran the other way.

Since that evening at the hospital I haven't talked to Kev's folks, and I have made a point of never riding by his old house. Then, last Monday, Clarise showed me a letter from Mr. Rubenstein.

"He's tried calling you for months now," she told me. "He's stopped by four different times. Oh, Alex, it's been so long. Don't you think you should talk to him? You were always so close with Kevin and his family."

Yeah, right, like I wanted to talk with the man about how I killed his son. I tore the letter into little pieces without reading it and flushed it. No way was I talking with him or Erin now. All my energy was concentrated on making the nightmare stop.

It had come to this: Sitting in the dark, in my closet with a loaded revolver, trying to figure out the best way to put a bullet in my brain.

I am seriously screwed.

But I'm also too whacked to know what to do, and I'm too afraid to pull the trigger. I lean my head against the wall.

Maybe tomorrow.

Maybe later.

Maybe.

# CHAPTER SIX

*Good evening ladies and gentlemen. Once again it's time for "Answer or Eat," the show brought to you by Bill and Clarise, the parents from hell. As the show's only contestant tonight, you'll sit still while Bill and Clarise hammer you with questions until you freak. Tonight's show is brought to you by Insanity, a common product here at the Anderson house, and a major ailment of most humans, everywhere. Our show begins with another useless dinner filled with some mind-numbing conversation. And now . . .*

I TRIED TO IGNORE CLARISE'S call to dinner, but I had just about decided that I might actually be hungry. I hadn't slept much last night. Today, I'd blown off school again and driven down to the river. There's a nice spot along the bank by a grove of cottonwoods. I liked it there. It was cool and didn't smell of dead fish. I stayed at the river all day, then came home.

And now, after three fun-filled hours staring at the same website, I'd stumbled downstairs into the den. Nobody there. There was, however, a light under the kitchen door. I pushed the door open. Bill, Clarise, and Jenny were seated at the kitchen table, a kitchen table covered with dishes full of what appeared to be home-cooked food.

Something wasn't right. There's a vase of fresh daisies and, yes, Clarise has actually cooked. What a treat—food that hasn't been exposed to sneezing delivery boys or microwaves. A real meal, and Clarise has outdone herself, too. Brisket, mashed potatoes, and honest-to-God brewed iced tea. She's even made three-bean salad. Something's definitely wrong. Three-bean salad is the dish she takes to funerals.

Jenny looked at me with a huge, fake smile, and tried a conversation starter.

"Hey, bro, what's up?"

Now I know something is in the works.

I sat down. Plates clinked. Bill poured me a glass of tea without saying anything. He just looked at me like, like he was sad. No one, other than Jenny, talked.

"All right. What's going on?" I grabbed a plate. "I know, you two are getting a divorce."

Clarise scowled at me and shook her head.

"No? Oh, then it must be her."

I pointed to Jenny, as she stuffed green beans in her mouth.

"Yep. That's it. Did some pinhead get her knocked up? I mean you gotta watch those horny fifteen-year-olds."

Clarise glared in my direction.

"Alex! That's horrible! How could you say such a thing?"

Jenny pouted but kept her mouth shut.

Bill looked at me: "What did you say?"

I dropped a glob of mashed potatoes on my plate.

"So, what's with dinner? Usually it's stale pizza and chips on the couch or a make-it-yourself sandwich."

"Well, son, I thought you'd like . . ."

Clarise looked at her napkin without finishing her sentence.

Something was seriously wrong.

"Son?"

Red Alert. Bill had puffed out his chest. He was using "the voice."

"Alex, your mother and I want to talk to you. We're very worried about you."

Here we go. Round three hundred and forty-seven.

*. . . And remember folks the winner of tonight's game gets to move on to our adulthood round!*

"I'd be fine if you'd just leave me alone for a while, okay?"

Clarise looked at me in disbelief.

"Honey, you've been depressed for months now. We're just concerned, and we want to prevent it from getting any worse." She'd opted for the ol' parental fear approach. It worked when I was in sixth grade. Now she'd dusted it off for an encore performance.

"I'm fine! Okay?"

Bill frowned. "It doesn't seem like you are—you have to admit your behavior lately has been a little extreme and erratic, don't you think? You spend all your time in your room. And we know you've been skipping school."

"Hey! That's a lie! I've been going! Who told you that?"

Clarise glared at me.

"Alex, the school called this afternoon. You haven't been to class in ages. You've only been there a few times since your suspension ended. And I know you've been erasing the calls and forging my name on notes. This is all a little much don't you think?"

She took a long drink of tea. Amazing, Clarise's smarter than I thought. Only I hadn't forged her name: I'd scanned her signature, then traced it. The whole thing worked pretty well.

So she was worried, and Bill thought I was being extreme. Extreme? When did Bill start worrying about being extreme? Okay, I hadn't done a lot in the past few months. But I did break Scott

Williams' jaw. Not everybody could say that. Who did Bill think he was—and why did he have to stick his nose in my business?

"Can't we talk about something else? Every time I turn around you guys are telling me how messed up I am."

I slammed my glass on the table. The tea splashed into the bowl of mashed potatoes. No one seemed to notice.

"Just give it a rest!"

Whoops. Tactical error. Bill's face went bright red. We're talking major chest-puffing action, too. Yes, he was definitely ticked off—he'd stopped eating.

"Now you listen here." He shook his fork at me.

"Let's talk about this later, okay? I have homework."

I stood up from the table ready to head to my room.

Bill grabbed my arm.

"Alex. You're not leaving. Stay right there. We need to talk."

He ushered me back to my chair.

"Okay! Okay! What gives?"

"Son, your mother and I love you very much. Today, well, today when your mom was putting your clothes up in your closet she found this." Bill reached under the table and pulled out a brown, wrinkled paper sack—my brown, wrinkled paper sack.

I felt the blood drain from my face.

"I . . . it's just some . . ."

"Alex. You had my pistol in your closet. And you loaded it."

"Look I was only looking at it. I wasn't going to . . ."

Bill shook his head. The weary sadness in his eyes told me he didn't believe me. "Oh, Alex. I know you're sad. Trust me, Trooper, I understand. Kev was a wonderful kid. Your mother and I miss him badly. We miss seeing you two together. But this." Bill laid the gun on the table. "This isn't the way to deal with the pain. You need some serious professional help, Alex."

My little sister reached across the table and tried to touch my hand. I jerked it away from her.

"Alex?" Jenny began to cry. "Please, I love you—please?"

I ignored her. My attention was focused on Bill and Clarise, the people I knew held my fate in their hands, though I couldn't figure out what kind of hand they were holding. "You're sending me to therapy twice a week. What more do you guys want?"

Clarise sat down her glass.

"Alex, we called the Wah-Sha-She Center."

Bill looked down at his food.

"What do you mean?" I asked.

"It's a treatment center for troubled youths," Bill said. "They handle eating disorders, drugs, alcohol, and . . . "

He didn't say it, but I knew the rest—and suicidal teenagers.

"I don't understand. You're talking about sending me to a treatment center? Why?"

Bill gave me a sad, twisted smile. "They have on-staff therapists and grief counselors. And between the three of us and Jan, your counselor, we think it would be a good idea for you."

"Yes," Clarise said. "We think you need some time to heal, away from here, away from all this bad energy. You need a chance to be around people who can devote all their time to helping you."

"I don't want to go," I said. "I've done what you asked. I go to therapy twice a week. All you have to do is leave me alone."

Clarise stood and moved next to me.

"That's not what we're talking about, honey. We're not going to take that chance. I'm not going to lose you."

Now Clarise had started crying, too. Jeez, what a nightmare. My parents had come seriously unglued. This sucked. They'd lost control. Bill hadn't called me, "Trooper" since I was in third grade.

I pushed my plate to the side.

"Look, I'm sorry. I'll put the gun back. I'm not going to kill myself." I faked a laugh. "I'll, I'll try to be better."

Bill wiped his face. He looked overwhelmed and sad.

"Alex. Son. I love you with all my heart. You're still my little boy. But right, now you need to be someplace else. You need intense therapy. You need to be where they can help you."

"What are you saying?" I looked at Bill, then Clarise.

"Since school ends on Friday, we've decided to send you to this center for the summer. We want to give you a chance to heal."

I threw my fork across the room.

"You mean you're locking me up in a place for screwed-up kids? It's not fair. I thought we'd agreed. You promised! I told you I just needed some space!"

YOU'VE PROBABLY FIGURED out by now, I got hosed. They tag-teamed me, and before I knew it, I was signed up for three months at some stupid center for troubled teens in southeastern Oklahoma.

Bill and Clarise said it had the best counselors in the state.

"They understand," Bill kept telling me. "They'll help you find the answers. It's not like a hospital. It's more like a camp. There's a lake and dorms, and, well, think of it as summer camp."

Yeah, right. The last time I went to summer camp I was ten. And the last time I was in any kind of house of worship it was a Jewish synagogue for Kev's funeral. You can bet I'm not doing that again. They knew I didn't want to leave home. I'd done my time with Therapy Chick. They'd promised.

I pushed myself away from the table and ran upstairs.

My whole world had been turned upside down. My best friend was dead. I wanted to kill myself. And my parents were sending me away for the summer for more therapy. I slammed my fists against the wall.

Game over. I'd lost—the bus would be here in the morning.

# PART TWO

# CHAPTER SEVEN

HELLO GANG—welcome to the Wah-Sha-She Center. I'm Mr. Redding, the assistant director. It is my pleasure to welcome you here—your home for the next three months. Grab your bags and follow me."

*Live from Crapville, America, it's Happy-Man, the dude who helps screwed-up teenagers prone to sitting in the dark and thinking about killing themselves. Yes, crime stoppers, unless you're drinking, stupid, or in prison, the Wah-Sha-She Center is the place to be.*

Now I know what the Trail of Tears was like. This guy, Redding, looks as if he just jumped off a Boy Scout recruitment poster—he has the shorts, he has the hat. He's not that tall. His hair is silvery, but there's not a whole lot of it. He's bouncing around, however, like he's downed way too many energy drinks.

We were corralled like cattle. I walked slowly down the steps of the bus. The fat kid ahead of me smelled of sweat and salami. His backside is about as wide as the back of Bill's sedan. He rambled on and on about being hungry. Behind me, a whining dork, so skinny he didn't throw a shadow, appeared to be dying of a breathing condition. Every time he took a step he wheezed. Next to him, some doofus from a town called Idabel was talking. He seemed hell-bent on using every cliché in the English language. He didn't even pronounce his own hometown right. He called it, "Ider-bell."

Well I didn't want to go to Ider-bell, and I didn't want to spend my summer at this hillbilly-church-therapy-save-your-soul-fix-the-screwed-up-teenager counseling center, either. Right now, I had both a sore butt and a dry throat, and I was surrounded by morons and misfits.

Get me out of here.


TRUTH BE TOLD, I'M SURPRISED we made it here at all. The ride down was three solid hours of the worst roads in Oklahoma. I felt every bump, pothole, and railroad track. To make matters worse, it rained and rained and rained—one of those unending, wet soggy rains that seeps into your very pores. By the time we arrived, there was so much mud the camp looked like a scene from the great flood—and it smelled like rotten fish.

The Wah-Sha-She Center sits just outside the town of Broken Bow, in the far most southeastern corner of Oklahoma. It's named for some old Indian medicine man who, I guess, did therapy on the side. The place is part summer camp, part treatment center. There's a large, central building, a smaller medical center, and several detached buildings scattered across a lawn that's trimmed as close as any golf course green I'd ever seen.

The students—yep, that's what we're called—live in two sets of cabins: males at one end, females at the other. Our cabins are down by a large grove of trees; the girls' are up a small hill, just past the cafeteria and the chapel.

The whole campus sits on the edge of a huge lake rimmed by

a forest of pine, oak, and red maples. You find your way from one place to the next by following the Wah-Sha-She Center's version of the yellow brick road, a wandering path that stretches from the central building to the cafeteria and the cabins. The camp makes a good first impression. It looked pretty—and pretty much like, what Bill likened it to, a summer camp. But looks can be deceiving, and should you forget where you are, you need only to walk behind the boat dock to find the large, chain-link fence and the waterproof video cameras. Then again, they were dealing with troubled teens.

Some of the inmates—okay, the students—called it a concentration camp. I wouldn't go that far *(Kev had told me about what his grandmother endured in one during the war)*, but I can tell you this: Wah-Sha-She is the last place in the world where I wanted to be right now.

"Okay kids. Drop your gear right there." Happy Man *(my name for Mr. Redding)* pointed to a swampy area next to the parking lot. "That's right. Good. Now, I'd like to introduce you to the director of our center, Mr. Hobson, and the rest of the staff."

He talked and talked. I realized any chance of him stopping any time soon was unlikely. In front of me, Lard Butt was whining about being hungry, his tennis shoes squishing and squeaking as he trudged through the rain-soaked grass. Hillbilly stomped by him.

"Boy howdy! Sure came a frog strangler! Just look at it, will ya?"

The kid couldn't open his mouth without croaking, like a backwoods, toothless jerk. I thought hillbillies were fiction, like unicorns, but this kid had proved me wrong. Man, Bill and Clarise must hate me to have sent me here—the place is full of losers, whiners, and weirdos.

We stopped walking. I saw three cabins—none as nice as the rest of the camp buildings. I stuck my head inside the first one; it smelled like mothballs and wet blankets. Happy Man kept talking.

". . . and remember we want the next three months to be the best of your summer. Our goal is, simply, to help you. So, if there's anything that I, or any of the staff here at camp, can do please don't hesitate to ask."

Screw this. Run right now, back to the highway. Thumb a ride to Stillwater. Make up with Bill and Clarise. Life could go back to normal.

". . . Now Trevor, Gus, JimBob, and Alex will be in Cabin F. Freddie, Matt, and Reese will be in Cabin G."

Happy Man wiped his forehead. A single water drop—from the branch above him—splashed his head. It dripped; he wiped.

"Okay guys. You have a couple of hours to meet your bunk mates, get your gear stowed, and take a look around. Oh yeah, Alex? Alex Anderson? Could I speak to you for a moment?"

Happy Man looked me right in the eye, so much for coming in under the radar.

I nodded. "Yeah? I'm Alex."

"Great, I just need a sec."

Now what? I hadn't even unpacked, and I'm already being forced to meet the management. Happy Man grabbed my hand and pumped it up and down.

"Hi! I've heard a lot about you. It's a pleasure to meet you. I've spoken with your parents, and I'd like the chance to talk with you one on one. Maybe after dinner?"

"Yeah, whatever."

"Good. Dinner is at five. Let me know if you need anything else."

*Maybe a harmonica?* Because I now know what it feels like to go to prison; I might as well learn to blow the blues while I'm here.


I STASHED MY GEAR and looked for the bathroom. Each cabin had two. They sat in the middle of the large, stark room that comprised my entire new home, up against one of the long walls. A fireplace and something approaching a kitchen filled one end of the room. On the other end, four bunks waited.

The bathroom smelled like bleach, fresh paint, and stale pee. The fumes were toxic. I whizzed, zipped my pants—just as the front door exploded. Six or seven kids stomped inside. Enter the Nerd Chorus, the official camp welcoming committee. After what seemed like a million "Hi! What's your name," I found my bunk. It was in the middle and smelled like the last person who had used it had a bladder control problem—but it was my bunk, just the same. Might as well get used to it.

Rick walked up to me. Each cabin has a counselor, and Rick was ours. A head taller than me, he was tanned with sandy hair and dark eyes. I'm sure the chicks grooved on him.

"Hey, I'm Rick." He stuck out his hand.

I gave him a quick shake and unzipped my bag.

Rick kept talking. "I'm the counselor assigned to this cabin. I'm here to help you and to keep you on task."

Yeah, right. I gave him my best "you're full of it" look.

"You're here to keep an eye on us, make sure we don't tick too many people off, and make sure we don't try to slip down the path to the girls' side. Right?"

"Maybe." He smiled, leaned closer, and lowered his voice to a whisper. "But Alex, you're stuck with me for the next three months. I'm not here to hurt you or to make your life miserable. But I don't put up with jerks, either. Know that. I'm here to help. But you have to decide that for yourself. So, let's try and get along and make the best of things. Okay?"

Okay, so he wasn't stupid. And right now he was in charge. So, we'd run his playbook. For now. I shoved my gear under the bed and plugged in my iPod.

> *Welcome to the hit show "Revenge of the Parents." Tonight see Bill and Clarise getting even with Alex. He's been exiled to Middle of Nowhere Oklahoma. Send your postcards to Alex Anderson, in care of Hell, Sixth Level, Moron Room.*

Rick slipped away to hang with some of the other kids. Looked around. There were people everywhere, and they had enough gear to fill a Wal-Mart. But that wasn't the worst part: Most of the idiots would eventually leave tonight, but the ones that remained, well, it was obvious they were members of Team Doofus—Trevor, Gus, and JimBob.

Or, as I liked to call them: Wheezer, Lard Butt, and Hillbilly.

I had lied to get the bottom bunk I wanted. Wheezer had gotten there first, but I told him I was afraid of heights and couldn't sleep on top. Wheezer shrugged and promptly crawled up top. Lard Butt cleared out a spot close to the refrigerator. Hillbilly stashed his stuff in the corner.

"Say Alex, ya' sure ya' don't want a peanut butter sandwich?"

Lard Butt, the human refrigerator, shoved two pieces of mangled bread coated with about six inches of greasy peanut butter towards me. I appreciated the gesture, but I wasn't that desperate—yet.

"Nawww. I think I'll just go look around." I said.

# CHAPTER EIGHT

SINCE THERE WAS NO way I wanted to hang with them, I went outside. The lake was about half a mile away, and I had plenty of time to kill. I sloshed through a black, muddy field—no dry spot anywhere thanks to the recent rain. It seemed strange to wade through an acre of thick, nasty sludge trying to find a big hole filled with even more water. But anything was better than Geek Patrol, Rick the counselor, or another interview with Happy Man. So I sacrificed my tennis shoes.

Once I was away from camp, the view got better: A pine forest rimmed an arm of Broken Bow Lake. The water was smooth, like a long, blue mirror. A soft breeze blew. Above me, a hawk circled. Nice view, but still a prison.

And it would take a lot more than a pretty view for me to want to stay here a week—much less three whole months.


I FOUND A STUMP AT THE TOP of a low rise, sat down, and scraped the slime off my shoes. I was reaching for a large stick when

I thought I heard someone scream, but I couldn't be sure. A few seconds later, I heard another scream, then loud, angry voices. I stood and ran down the hill. About two hundred yards in front of me, a hot blonde in shorts and a T-shirt was ranting at a tall muscular guy with a face like a snake. From where I stood, it looked like they knew each other, but the girl wasn't happy. She and the guy were face to face—and they looked ready to rumble.

Snake Face waved his arms. "Come on Rachel, it's just a kiss. I drove all the way up here just to see you."

"I didn't ask you to come!"

Snake Face leaned in for the girl.

She pushed him away. He leaned towards her again.

"What's the matter with you?"

"I told you before. It's over, Danny. Now stop!"

With that, Blondie pushed Snake Face back—hard, but he refused to take the message, and he slithered in for a third try.

"Stooooop it, Danny!" The girl stomped her foot, splashing black mud everywhere. "How many times do I have to say it. It's over. We talked about this. I don't know why you came! What does it take to get it through that thick skull of yours?"

*Oh, so Snake Face has a name, Danny. Actually, he looks more like, a Richard, as in Dick.*

"Guess you don't remember *us*, huh?"

"Yeah, I remember," she said, "but like I told you, that's in the past. I don't know you anymore, and I don't want *this* anymore. I'm sorry; you came all this way for nothing."

Lacking anything better to do, I walked towards them. And as I did I got this strange feeling in my gut, an out-of-this-world, freaky type of feeling. Something pulled me towards the Blonde. It sounds crazy, but I swear to you, it was like, well, I needed to be near her.

As I came closer, the girl started to calm down. She turned her head. Was she looking at me? Did she see me? I couldn't tell. She turned back around and gave it one last try.

"Look Danny, I don't want to fight. I'm not trying to hurt you."

"Not trying to hurt me?" Danny's face glowed red. "Not trying to hurt me? Rachel! We were together for like a year. Then out of the blue you call me and tell me it's over? What's up with that? What's changed?"

"You changed."

I was about fifty feet away at this point. By now, I figured the only way Danny knew how to talk was to scream. I always thought that was weird. People will get all mad and yell at each other at the top of their lungs, screaming stuff they would never want anyone else to know, but making sure everyone hears them.

I climbed up on a large rock and faked like I was resting from the hike. Snake Face leaned over and whispered something to Rachel. She went nuclear. Got right in his face. Stomped her feet. Waved her arms. Basically exploded. She was a sight to behold.

"Stupid? No, I'm not stupid! I wasn't stupid when I saw you pawing Melissa Peters! I wasn't stupid when I saw you flirting with Ashley North, and I did not imagine you and Karen Larson doing the horizontal bop on the pep bus, did I?"

Snake Face snarled. His eyes folded into tiny slits. The left side of his mouth twisted into a thin, tight line. "I told you I was sorry. What more do you want? Just give me another chance."

Snake Face reached for the girl again, grabbed her by the arm, and twisted. She pulled back, so he yanked harder. She pulled back again, and he grabbed something from her wrist. It looked like a slender, silver charm bracelet.

"Give me that back," Rachel hissed.

Danny dangled the bracelet high above the girl's hands.

"You and your freaking numbers!"

Rachel jumped trying to reach the bracelet so she could pull it out of his hand.

"Stop it! Give it back. That's from my grandmother!"

Snake Face lowered his arm. He pushed Rachel backwards.

"Yeah I know," he said. "This stupid thing means more to you than anything I ever gave you!"

And with that, Danny broke the bracelet in two, twisted the links, and in one swift motion broke them again.

"There!" He tossed the pieces in the lake. "You want it so bad— go swim for it!"

Honestly, I was amazed. I'd never seen a guy be so mean, so vindictive. I watched the girl, Rachel, grow still and smolder. She reminded me of Jenny: pretty and curvy but capable of serious combustion. I decided I would just sit back and watch. It looked to be the best drama on any TV or movie screen in the area. One thing's for certain: I wasn't going to get tied up in this fight.

The girl exploded.

"I hate you." She choked back tears. "I never thought I'd say it, but I hate you! All you are is mean. You wanna know why we're over? That's why! Because you're not a nice person anymore. You're mean and cruel, and you only think about yourself."

I could tell she had more to say, but she was busy trying hard not to bawl. From where I sat, it looked like the words weren't coming out quite the way she planned.

"I don't ever want to see you again!"

She whipped around and started to walk away.

Snake Face grabbed her arm and yanked her towards him. In one swift motion, he pulled back his hand and slapped her hard in the face. The force knocked her to her knees and brought me to my feet. I jumped off the stump and started to run—towards them. I could tell the girl was shocked the guy had hit her, but she recovered faster than I would have thought possible. I hadn't gotten very far when the girl pulled back a fist and hammered Snake Face right in the balls.

"Don't you ever hit me again!" she yelled.

Snake Face dropped to the ground, groaning and moaning as if he was dying. I slowed down. Both of them were still pretty mad. I wasn't sure if there would be a round two. Jeez. I'd been in a lot of fights, but I'd never seen a guy slug a girl.

Snake Face reached up and tried to grab Rachel by the hair.

She batted his arm away and stepped out of reach.

"Stop trying to hurt me!"

Danny rolled over and fell face first into the mud. By this time, I was only a few feet from Rachel. She turned and stomped towards me. Somehow Danny managed to grab her once more with a dirty hand.

"Listen!" He screamed. "I'm tired of this!"

And with that, he leapt to his feet and lightning quick slapped her again. For a second, I was stunned. I cringed as Rachel grabbed the side of her face in pain. Snake Face pushed her again and brought his hand back for a third time. He never got the chance to connect.

I grabbed his hand.

"I don't think so. Where I'm from, we don't hit girls."

I pushed him back, turned, and helped Rachel up off the ground. But lover-boy wasn't giving up. He followed, slipping and sliding. I figured I was screwed. I'd only been at camp a few hours and already I'd stepped into the middle of a fight. I hoped the authorities would understand. I might be messed up, but I still had my own code of honor. And I was not going to sit by and watch some freak whale on a girl.

Rachel held tight to my hand, and we walked up the hill.

WE'D GONE ABOUT FIFTY FEET when Snake Face caught up with us. He threw a punch and nailed me on the side of my face. My feet left the ground, and it was my turn to be wallowing in the mud.

"Get up!"

He stood over me and snorted, like a mad bull.

I sat up and flipped the mud off my hands.

"Get lost, loser. She told you to leave her alone."

He leveled a kick, but I caught his foot and dumped him on his butt. While he rolled around in the muck, trying to get his bearings, I looked into the eyes of one pretty *(and still very ticked off),* petite steamroller in a sunny yellow tee.

"Oh! Oh! I'm sorry. Are you okay?"

It took me a moment to take in the whole image, but standing there, against a bright blue sky, was one of the prettiest girls I'd seen in a long time—hazel eyes, blonde hair, and full, red lips. And curves—soft, lush curves—she was, simply, beautiful.

"Ahhh, yeah. I'm fine." I scraped the mud off my jeans and stuffed my shirt back into my pants. "What was that all about? You okay?" I rubbed my hands together, trying to remove some of the excess mud.

"I'm fine. That was my boy . . . my ex-boyfriend."

Rachel grabbed a red bandanna out of her back pocket and started to wipe the mud off my face.

"I've tried breaking up with him for weeks," she said, "but he keeps stalking me. He drove all the way up from Texas. Then, today, well, you saw."

I nodded. "Are you sure you're all right?"

"I'm okay. He just caught me off guard. You can bet that won't happen again."

Before she could say anything more, Snake Face returned, like a monster from a cheap horror movie. He was covered in black mud, and the spots on his face—the ones not covered in gunk—were now bright red. The veins on the side of his neck bulged as if they were about to pop. I'd say he was four inches taller than me, pale and slim, with massive biceps from more than one hay-hauling trip. He was way beyond mad but trying hard to hide it, acting instead like he was all worried about Rachel.

"Hey Rachel, honey, are you okay?"

Rachel gave him the meanest go-to-hell-do-not-pass-go-do-not-collect-two-hundred-dollars look I'd ever seen.

"No. I am not. Not after you just hit me. Get away from me or I will call the police. I'm sorry I ever met you!"

His eyes narrowed. "I said I was sorry. You just made me mad. It wouldn't have happened if *you* hadn't ticked *me* off. Honestly, you're the one who should apologize. Now, come on honey, let's go."

Danny reached for Rachel. Without thinking, I slid between them. "Hey! Are you deaf? She said, 'Beat it.' So get lost!"

"Why don't you mind your own business?" Danny reached for Rachel yet again. I pushed him back. Don't get me wrong. I'm definitely not the hero-type, but my life was basically over so what did I have to lose?

At least that's what I was telling myself as I stood there, but honestly, something else was at work. Inside I had this feeling in my gut—like I said earlier, a weird and strange pull. I knew without a doubt that I was supposed to be there, protecting Rachel. I couldn't help it. Something drew me to this girl, and no hay-bale-toting Bubba with bulging neck veins was going to keep me away.

I pushed Danny back with a chest bump.

"Beat it!"

Danny gave me his best alpha male look.

"Make me, pencil neck."

Fair enough. Growing up with Kev I'd learned to appreciate the fine art of trash talk. But somehow, anything this guy said was a whole different story. I pushed him backwards. He stumbled.

Round two of Snake Face versus Alex had started.

I pointed at him. "Bring it."

I sounded a lot more confident than I felt. I told myself no one could tell, but I knew I was about to piss in my pants. What was wrong with me? What was wrong with my life? I'd been in southeastern Oklahoma for three hours and already it looked like I was about to get my butt kicked.

Danny shoved me.

I shoved back.

"Look," I said, "just leave her . . ."

He took a long, slow swing. I feinted left. He overstepped and fell headfirst into a slimy pile of rotten black crud. Behind me, Rachel yelled. I looked down at his face—he looked like a catfish that had been on the bank too long, muddy and pale.

"Beat it, redneck!"

Snake Face flung a fistful of mud at my face, jumped up, and nailed me with a right cross to the chin. I staggered back but managed to get one last swing off as he grabbed Rachel by the arm.

"I'll get you later, Rachel. You'll regret this."

Rachel yanked herself free. And before I knew what was happening, Snake Face popped me in the eye with a muddy fist. I fell backwards, but not before I landed a punch to the right side of his head. For a big guy, he didn't have much balance. Once again, he was back in the mud.

"I'm gonna kick your butt, dork!" he yelled.

I snarled. "Not from there."

He struggled to his feet. We stood face to face. I was a mess, but he was covered head to toe in black mud, like a walking oil slick. Rachel shoved herself between us.

"Just leave! Okay, Danny?" Her hazel eyes blazed with renewed fury. "Leave. Now. Before you get hurt."

"Listen, you . . . " He pushed her again.

"If you don't leave now, I'm going to call the police, then I'm going straight to Mr. Redding and tell him you hit me—*and this time I have a witness.*"

I could tell she meant what she said. Snake Face seemed to realize it, too, because he dropped his fists.

"Fine! I don't need you in my life anyway." He turned and started up the hill, only to stop, turn around, and face me.

"You can have her. Who'd want her anyway?"

He waved a muddy hand at Rachel.

"You make me sick!"

He took a few more steps and disappeared behind a grove of trees. I turned to Rachel and looked her straight in the eyes with more than a little disbelief.

"That guy is the biggest jerk I've ever met. Are you sure he was your boyfriend?"

"Yeah, he didn't used to be like that, but something changed a few months ago. Something happened at home, and he started hanging out with some older guys and getting into trouble. I don't know what all he's into now, but he wasn't violent before. All I know now is I'm sorry I ever went out with him."

"I'm sorry you did, too."

I touched her face where he'd hit her. She jerked away.

"Hey, it's okay." I touched her cheek again. There was an angry red blotch on it. "Let me look at you. You got popped pretty good."

"I'm fine."

Rachel tried to turn away from me. Her voice sounded raspy —and she was having trouble breathing.

"You sure you're all right?"

"Yeah. Sometimes it's hard for me to catch my breath, especially after dealing with the likes of him."

She leaned toward me and put both her arms on my shoulders. She took a deep, full breath. After a few seconds, she began to look more relaxed.

"Oh, hey, I didn't even thank you for rescuing me."

I looked into her big, beautiful eyes and returned the smile.

"No need. It was nothing."

"No it wasn't. He's bothered me for weeks. Then we started fighting and . . . and I saw you there on the hill."

She wiped more mud off me, then herself, then glanced at her wrist, like she was seeing it for the first time.

"He broke my bracelet!"

Her eyes darted back and forth, and she started to panic again, breathing heavy and growing pale. She looked like she'd just lost her last friend.

"I can't lose that bracelet. It's all I have from my grandmother."

"I'm pretty sure it's gone."

I pointed to the spot where I'd seen Danny toss it into the lake.

"He knew what that bracelet meant to me."

"Look, I'm sorry. I can wade in the water if you want me to try and look for it."

Without giving me an answer, Rachel stepped into the lake. She started to push the water back with her hands. Then she tried to strain it with her fingers. Neither worked. Finally, she leaned over and tried running her fingers through the muddy bottom. That proved no more productive than her seining efforts had. She shook her head; she looked about to cry.

"No. It's gone. Gone forever."

In a lame attempt to console her, I tried running my hands along the bottom of the lake, but I was no more successful than she had been. I stood and wiped the black gunk off of me for the fiftieth time just as a light clicked on in my brain. I turned towards her.

"What do you mean, you saw me up on the hill? You knew I was up there all that time?"

Rachel nodded. She wiped her face with her bandanna.

"Yeah. It's weird, too. Right after I saw you. I had this feeling. I knew I could trust you—I knew you wouldn't let Danny hurt me."

The hair stood up on the back of my neck. I wanted to respond, but I wasn't sure what to say, so I faked it.

"About your bracelet, maybe we could get you another one?"

Rachel shook her head.

"No. My grandmother is dead. That was the last thing I had from her."

Both her voice and her face were so sad, I didn't give it a second thought. I just dropped to my knees in the lake water and started digging. My hands and fingernails filled with more black crud.

I didn't even notice.


AN HOUR LATER, SOAKED and still empty-handed, we slogged back up the hill. I wanted to say something reassuring to her, but didn't know where to begin. A million questions streamed through my mind. I wanted to ask her where her cabin was, what group she ate dinner with, what she'd be doing tomorrow, and when we could get together again.

But in the end, I didn't say anything. As we neared camp, a bell started ringing. "What the heck is that?" I asked.

Rachel giggled.

"Oh that. We call that the prayer bell."

She headed toward the cafeteria, giving me a little side glance.

"They ring it when it's time for vespers."

"Vespers?"

"Just think of it as a short church service."

"Great. Just great. I'm wet and covered in who knows how many layers of mud. I almost got my butt kicked. I'm stuck with three roommates from hell, and now I have to go to church."

Rachel grinned. "Well the day wasn't a total loss."

"Huh?"

"You met me."

She turned those awesome hazel eyes on me, and, for a couple of seconds, I didn't know what to say. We started toward the chapel, but then Rachel turned and faced me again; she looked like she was puzzling over something important.

"Sorry, I didn't introduce myself. I'm Rachel. Rachel Clark."

She shook my hand.

Then she frowned. "And what do I call you, my brave sir?"

I'm not sure whether it was the look in her eyes or the goofy way she asked, but once again words failed me. I just stood there dripping mud and looking stupid; I'd almost given up on ever speaking again when something jump-started me.

"Ahhh, Alexxx." I stuttered. "Call me Alex."

# CHAPTER NINE

NO DOUBT ABOUT IT, even covered in gunk, Rachel was a girl to reckon with. I walked behind her, a silly grin on my face. I had told her I didn't know my way around the camp, but, really, I just liked watching her butt sway.

"You doin' okay up there?"

"Yeah, I'm fine."

Rachel walked a few more feet, turned, and gave me a look. Oh man, she knew exactly what I was thinking . . . and looking at. My face turned fire engine red.

"So is this the first time you've ever seen a girl's bum? You know, we're all made pretty much the same way."

She glared at me, then turned and trotted toward the cafeteria. My face felt as if it were on fire. Rachel turned back to look at me once more. This time her face was tense.

"You guys are all alike. You have only one thing on your mind."

"Hey, sorry! I was just . . . "

She started to run—away from me, as fast as she could. I knew I deserved to be blown off. Part of me wanted to crawl down a hole, but, if I was being honest, I had to admit the other part of me liked watching her, even if it made her mad. I made a quick decision and stepped up my jog, until I pulled even with her again.

"Look, I'm sorry. I wasn't trying . . ."

Rachel's face softened.

"Oh, it's okay," she said.

I stopped in my tracks.

"Are you, are you still mad?"

Rachel turned and shook her head.

"No. I was just teasing you."

I faked like I was shocked.

"No fair! And just so you know, I'm thinking about a lot of stuff right now."

Rachel's face clouded.

"Oh yeah and what's that?"

"Food, that's what."

"Alex!"

Rachel grabbed a clump of muddy grass and nailed me in the head with it, catching me off guard. I lost my balance, and, once again, I was on my back in the mud. Honestly, pigs don't wallow in mud as much as I did that day.

"Oh, oh, Alex I'm sorry. Truly I am. Are you okay?"

I held up a muddy hand. "Yeah, I'm fine. I love this stuff. Here, help me up."

She grabbed my hand and pulled. The two of us were far from presentable, especially me, but we made it to the chapel, a square, squat white-washed building with a cross above the door.

The bell ringing stopped. Outside the chapel, the entire Wah-Sha-She population stood in one long line—it reminded me of half-price, chili-dog night at a SHS football game.

Rachel looked up at me.

"So, do you *really* like my . . .?"

"What?" I said, feigning cluelessness.

"Well, you said . . . do you think I'm . . . ?"

**67**

"Huh? What are you talking about?"

"Alex, you know."

Now she was the one all flustered, and I was the one cool and controlled. I knew what she wanted me to say, but it was more fun to watch her sweat.

"Let me put it this way: You are, most definitely, not ugly."

She rolled her eyes.

"Ahhh, thanks. It's nice to know I'm not . . . ugly."

I scratched my head, like I was Hillbilly thinking real hard.

"Yeah. That's an established fact, a major fact, a serious fact. The kind of fact that is factually a fact, in fact."

She smiled and shook her head.

"So are you planning on sitting with anyone at dinner?" she asked.

I looked up at the sky, like now I had to think about it. This time, I rolled my eyes, too.

"Hmmm, I don't know. I heard about this real hot girl with strange tastes in guys. But I'm having second thoughts. Seems she has a mud fetish."

I looked up. I looked down. I looked up again, as if seeking guidance from above.

"I guess eating dinner with this girl would be okay, but if I'm going to hang with her, I'd better start carrying paper towels."

Rachel laughed and grabbed my arm; she pulled me to the side of the chapel, towards a leaky water faucet.

"Hurry, we only have a couple of minutes."

She turned the faucet handle and a stream of cold water splashed my feet. She whipped out her bandanna again, and, after some serious scrubbing, my face was back to normal. She started to laugh.

"Now, don't you feel better?"

"Yeah. I'm great, but my butt is still sore from the bus ride. I've already been in a fight with a total stranger. I'm soaking wet, and everything, except for my face, is covered in mud. And as if that weren't bad enough, for the last hour, I've been trying to defend a strange girl who mopes over broken jewelry and has a serious affinity for mud. So, yeah, I'm fine. Thanks for asking. How about you?"

There was this long pause. Then, just when she turned to go, I took her hand and smiled.

"Actually, I'm fine."

"You sure?"

Her face was sort of twisted in doubt.

"Yep. Just fine."

# CHAPTER TEN

RACHEL LYNN CLARK stood just shy of five-foot-three. She had bright hazel eyes, blond hair, and, well, she was beautiful. But that was just the physical stuff. Over the next week I learned that she was as smart as Kev, loved to laugh, and had read enough books to fill two or three libraries. The best part was she liked me. And that, at this point in my life, was almost too good to be true.

It was difficult to imagine anyone liking me. My own parents didn't much like me. I lived in two different worlds: Comfortable around Rachel. (*I liked being with her, and when I was with her things didn't seem so bad.*) But left alone, dark and alienated.

I'd tried to lose the dark side. I avoided being alone. And when I had to be alone, I tried thinking about anything else—lawn mower engines, buckets of paint, and irritating songs on the radio. Nothing helped. It was like somebody else was driving my head.

*Yes, once again, it's time to play "Drive Alex Crazy," the studio game in which you, the audience, gets to screw*

*up an already screwed-up human. Watch as Alex struggles
with the past, while he tries to make sense of the present and
all the while trying to win a host of fabulous prizes.*

I SAT BY THE LAKE, beneath a huge maple tree. Rick, the counselor, on one side of me. Mr. Redding on the other. We were having
what they called "a rap session." I called it "hell under a tree."

"Alex, we've been here for more than an hour and haven't ac-
complished much," Mr. Redding said. "Believe it or not, we do care.
We're trying to help you."

I scowled.

"It doesn't seem that way. I was only here two days before you
started shoving pills down my throat and had wonder boy here . . ."
I pointed to Rick. ". . . as my around-the-clock guard. I feel like a
criminal."

Rick patted my arm.

"Alex, it's not like that. You see, when we get a student who has
had the difficulties that you have had, well . . . "

Mr. Redding interrupted him.

"The truth is Alex that Rick is paid to watch you. And you're
not being fair. You were on suicide-watch, because you threatened
it at home. You had a gun hidden in your bedroom closet. What
would you do if you were in our position?"

I looked at my feet. I hadn't thought of it from their perspective.

"I don't know," I said, "but I'd try to be a little more understanding. I'm not dead, am I?"

Mr. Redding smiled.

"No, son, you're still with us. And we want to keep it that way.
From the reports I hear you've impressed a lot of people. Mrs. Al-
lison loves your pottery, and Rick says you're kind and you try to help
others. Those are positive signs. I also hear you've met Rachel."

He paused and looked right into my face.

"What do you think of her?"

Amazing. I must be under satellite surveillance. How did they know about Rachel?

"Ahhh, yeah, we met. I also met her ex-boyfriend, too."

"Yes, I wanted to talk to you about Danny," Rick said. "Rachel told me how you defended her against him. She was very impressed."

Did I hear that right? She was impressed?

"She, she said that? I figured I'd just gotten myself in a jam fighting on my first day here."

Rick and Mr. Redding laughed.

"It could have gone that way," Mr. Redding said, "had Rachel not explained everything. The original intent of this meeting with you was to discuss that exact problem."

He paused and wiped his face.

"But Rachel explained the situation, and, well, let's just say we see things a little differently now."

I nodded. "So I'm not in trouble?"

"Not this time. I look at it like this: you were defending a fellow student from a violent outsider. We respect and appreciate that."

"But there's something I don't understand," I said.

"What's that?" Mr. Redding asked.

"Why is Rachel here? She's normal. She's not crazy. She's not fighting food or drugs or booze. She's not suicidal. What gives?"

"Rachel is here for other reasons." Mr. Redding said.

I looked at Rick for a better answer.

"We can't tell you a lot, Alex. But you're right. Rachel isn't here for any of the things you mentioned."

"She's here for her health," Mr. Redding said. "Without going into too much detail, Rachel is here for medical reasons."

Mr. Redding patted my arm, as if he understood my frustration at their non-answer answers.

"I've known her family for years," Mr. Redding said. "I've watched Rachel grow up. You should get to know her. She's an amazing young woman."

I felt myself smile at the thought of her.

"She's very pretty, but that doesn't seem like enough of a handicap for her to be here."

Rick laughed.

"You're right, Alex. She's not a resident. She's a volunteer. She said she wanted to come and soak up some sun and help."

He made the Boy Scout salute. I wasn't convinced.

"On my honor," Rick said. "Now, don't you think we should talk about you?"

Maybe, I was still mad, but, right then, I didn't want to talk, and I guess it showed on my face.

"Can't we let this go? I have talked to you. Weren't you listening?"

Mr. Redding scowled. Now he seemed mad, but, at that point, I didn't care. He stood and motioned to Rick.

"Okay, let's adjourn early this time," Mr. Redding said, "but remember Alex, we can't help you if you won't talk to us. You have to engage. You have to participate in your own treatment."

I yawned.

"Yeah sure, just so long as I take your little pills. Right?"


AFTER MY "RAP" SESSION, I skipped art class. The warmth of the sun on my face and the touch of soft grass under my feet felt good. I leaned my head back against a tree. I was trying to calm down and forget about people, especially the people who wanted to pry off the top of my head and look inside. I sat quietly for a while. A shadow fell on me and, above me, a soft voice spoke.

"Hey handsome, you eaten yet?"

I opened my eyes. Rachel stood over me. Sunlight sparkled through her hair.

"Where did you come from?"

"Over there." She pointed to one of the girl cabins. "I saw you sitting here. Thought I'd come pester you. You okay?"

"Yeah, I guess."

"You don't look okay. What's up?"

"Nothing. Just had a blast at my rap session. I'm fine. Perfect."

Rachel frowned. She knew I was lying.

"I don't get you, Alex. For a while now, I've tried to get you to tell me what's wrong. I know there's something, but you've avoided me. I saw you talking to Rick and Mr. Redding. They're great. But they looked mad when they finished with you. What did you say to them? Why are you always so mad?"

I picked up a rock and tossed it towards the lake.

"It's nothing."

Rachel leaned toward me.

"Have I made you mad? Is that it? I thought you liked me? I mean, that day by the lake you protected me in a way no one ever has. You fought Danny. And you didn't even know who I was. And when I'm around you, I feel safe and happy. But when I try to talk to you about something that's obviously bothering you, you shut me out."

I gave her a lame smile.

"Hey, at least Danny's stayed gone."

"Alex, I don't want to talk about Danny. I want to talk about you."

*Jeez. Why couldn't everyone give me some space?* I wasn't bothering anyone. I was just sitting alone. I turned toward her.

"It's nothing. Okay? I just don't want to talk right now."

"Sometimes it can help, talking to someone who'll listen. Whatever is eating at you can't be that bad. Seriously, nobody's bleeding; nobody's dead."

Maybe it was what she said. Or maybe, how she said it. Whatever it was, I lost it. For a split second I wasn't at a counseling center. Instead, I was at home, in the kitchen, hearing Bill and Clarise tell me it was time to get over Kev's death.

I threw my arms up in the air.

"Dead? What do you know about death? You have everything,

Rachel—beauty, brains. You're just here at camp to feel better. Your friends are alive. You can call them or see them anytime you want. Look, I don't want to talk. Okay?"

I turned away from her.

"Alex? What's wrong? What did I say?"

I turned back to her. My insides boiled.

"What is so hard to understand? It's my problem, and I'll deal with it! It's none of your damn business. Just leave me alone!"

The veins on my neck throbbed. I felt sick. I knew she was mad, but I didn't want to look at her.

"Everyone's trying to get into my head! I'm sick of it! I wish everyone would just leave me alone! I wish I'd never set foot in this place! I wish I'd never met Kev! I wish I never knew him! I'm sorry, okay? Sorry I ever met him! Is that what you want to hear? Go. Away. Can't you see I don't want to talk to you?"

I couldn't believe all that rushed out of my mouth. I'd lost control. Somebody else was pushing the buttons and pulling the levers. Or maybe I was evil—I'd killed one person, maybe I was just possessed or sick. I covered my head. I didn't want to see the look on her face.

> *We interrupt our scheduled program for a news bulletin: Alex Anderson has just made a total and complete idiot of himself. Chances for recovery look slim. Tropical Storm Alex struck at exactly 3:15 this afternoon, destroying all human feelings in its path. Stay tuned to this channel for more emergency information.*

"Alex? Why?"

Rachel's voice was little more than a whisper.

Slowly, I uncovered my eyes and peered through my fingers. Rachel stood over me, with both hands on her hips. Her face had gone white, like expensive marble. But her hazel eyes still shined—as if an unnatural light illuminated them from behind. It was unreal. She stood still for a second, then she leaned down and pushed her face right into mine.

"Look, mister I don't know what your problem is, but I don't need this!" She poked my chest with her finger. "And I don't deserve you yelling at me! You don't want to talk? Fine! You want to go through the rest of the summer playing the part of the distant loner mad at the world, well, that's fine with me, too!"

She took a breath. I could tell I had lost her.

Her eyes narrowed.

"But when the time comes when you're all alone and wishing you had someone to listen to you, don't come looking for me. Got it?"

She stood up, and for a second I was blinded by the bright sunlight that rushed into the void she'd left behind.

"Rachel, I'm . . ."

She'd heard enough from me.

"You're so smart, but look at you! Do you think you're the only one who's ever had a problem? Ever been in pain? Well, I hate to tell you, but you're not! There are a bunch of us out there. But we get up every morning and try to make it through another day. Unlike you, we don't give up. Yes, life is hard. It's like taking college classes when you're in grade school. Most of the time the only difference between the winners and losers is simply that the winners are the ones who refuse to give up, who refuse to wrap themselves in a blanket of self pity and check out."

She took a deep breath.

"Alex, I'm sorry about your problem—whatever it is! And I'm sorry you're so sad. Real sorry. But mostly, I'm sorry, because you can't see the help that's right in front of you. You won't let go of this wall of pain you've built around yourself. There might as well be a moat between us, because you've pulled up the bridge. If you could just see that you're not the only one who's ever been hurt! You could see that other people care about you!"

I was shocked.

I hadn't had someone talk to me like that since the night of Kev's death at the hospital. "Rachel, I'm sorry. I didn't mean . . . "

"I was only trying to help, but no, you're too self-absorbed. You wouldn't listen. You . . . "

Before she could say another word, I grabbed her arm and turned her to face me.

"Look, I said 'I was sorry.' If you'd stand still long enough, you might see that I'm trying."

Rachel drew herself up; she looked almost haughty. With a toss of her hair, she put me in my place.

"You are the one who copped an attitude! You are just as bad as Danny! Just leave me alone. I'm sorry I ever talked to you!"

I stood there speechless, like a moron. Before I could say anything, she turned and walked away.

I sat back down. Well, we wouldn't be hanging out any time soon. And that made part of me even sadder. That part of me wanted to run after her and make her understand how I had come to be the way I was. But the other part of me was furious. I didn't give a damn if I'd upset her or if I'd never see her again. I mean, come on, I wasn't bothering anyone.

I just wanted to be left alone.


I GUESS I SAT THERE about an hour, long enough for my butt to go numb. Sitting wasn't helping, so I stood, dusted off my pants, and started for the cafeteria—prepared to begin my new role as a social loner. Fate, however, had other plans: a second dose of Rachel.

I watched her stomp towards me in utter disbelief, figuring she was headed to see someone behind me. I looked over my left shoulder to see who it could be. There was no one. When I turned back around, she stood in front of me. She could have knocked me over with a blade of grass.

"Do you want to tell me about your problem, or do I leave? It's your call."

"Huh?" My head spun, like a wind turbine in an F4 tornado. "I thought you were mad? And you did leave. Remember? You said I was a jerk. You said you weren't going to talk to me anymore; you said I don't . . . "

She gave me the exact look Clarise does when I'm being stupid. The "why are you such an idiot" mixed with a little of "don't-mess-with-me-because-I'm-ten-times-smarter-than-you-and-could-kill-you-with-one-finger" look. It wasn't a look you wanted to get more than once. I had to admit Rachel had the look down. Rachel could stare down Satan. No wonder Danny split so fast the other day.

She took a couple of steps towards me.

"So are we talking or are you going to opt for moping? 'Cause this is your last chance, buddy."


OKAY, JUST SO YOU KNOW, I'm not stupid. Bill and Clarise didn't raise a dummy. I knew I didn't want her to go. So I begged——a lot. And, yes, there might have been some groveling, too.

"Yeah . . . ahh . . . look (*I didn't say it was eloquent groveling*), Rachel please stay. I'm sorry; I didn't mean . . . "

I hadn't stammered so much since Bill busted me for cruising the porn channels of our cable service. Rachel's face softened. Slowly, the flames in her eyes cooled to a wet, soft glisten. She went from inferno to limpid pool. She touched my hand.

"Alex. I'll be honest. I really, really like you. You stood up for me. No one's ever done that for me, and I'll never forget it. Talk to me, okay? I can't help it; I care about you.

"I thought you were different," she said. "And, well, I liked it here because you were here. I don't want to lose that."

Her confession made me feel like a louse.

"Rachel, I'm sorry. Honest. I didn't mean to scream at you. My head's just messed up."

Rachel pulled me to her. I looked into her soft, gentle face, and, slowly, the bad feelings faded.

"It's okay. If you don't want to talk now, I'll listen anytime. But, please, don't push me away again," she said.

I nodded. She was close enough I could smell her hair—peaches and vanilla. My head spun as I looked at her.

"It's weird, okay? I mean, after you hear the whole story, you might not want anything to do with me."

Rachel smiled, a knowing little smile.

"Trust me?"

"I do. I just don't want to talk. Okay? I mean I'm glad you're here, but not now."

Rachel nodded. "It's your loss."

I was glad she'd finally let it drop.


I OBVIOUSLY DIDN'T KNOW Rachel well, because not even a minute later, she was back and trying again. The girl had some nerve.

"Does it have anything to do with a boy named Kevin?"

My eyes all but blew out of my head.

"Huh?"

"You heard me. Does your problem involve a boy named Kevin?"

The snakes were back. My guts churned. Now I was the one shocked. I was sure my chin had hit the dirt.

"How in the hell do you know about Kev?"

Rachel looked me straight in the eyes, willing me to come clean.

And I gave up. Exhausted from a year of keeping it all inside, I couldn't muster the energy to keep silent any longer.

"All right," I said, "but it's sick. It happened last year, and I guess I'm not dealing with it well, but I still don't know how you know about Kev."

Rachel took my hand. "Alex you just don't get it. I knew about Kevin, because you've said the name 'Kev' over and over for the past couple of days. And just a few minutes ago you screamed something about 'wishing you had never met Kevin.' And every time you talk about him, you always look so sad. So it's obvious you knew someone named Kevin, and it's obvious something bad happened."

I looked at her dumbstruck.

"I found this gun and loaded it and kept it in my closet in this paper sack, which was a stupid idea, and, well, that's why I'm here."

"What else do you know about me?"

She moved closer.

"Well, I didn't know that what had happened was that horrible. What I do know is you're handsome, and you're sweet—most of the time. I also know you're brave and you're upset about this Kevin-person. I'm pretty sure you're angry and hurt, too. You're mad at your parents. And you don't want to be here—or don't think you should be here. Believe me that's obvious."

If she knew all that, why bother talking?

"Is that all?"

Rachel laughed. "Pretty much. But there is one more thing."

"Yeah, what?"

She squeezed my hand and gave me a little grin.

"I'm not going to let you go, until you talk to me."

# CHAPTER ELEVEN

S O I LAID OUT the whole ugly story. When I came to the part about how I watched Kev die she cried. That surprised me. I figured the details would make her sick and she'd leave, but I was wrong. She stayed. She said she wanted to know everything, so we skipped my archery class and vespers.

Later, after the dining room had emptied, we snuck through the back door and nabbed a sandwich for each of us. Rachel ate hers like it was her last meal.

"Aren't too many boys I'd choose over dinner." She slugged down a cold soda. "You should feel special."

"I do. Just promise you won't bite a hunk out of me."

"Well, then, you'd better keep talking."

We walked to the lake. The sun had dropped behind the trees, and the sky was painted in purple and yellow. Slashes of red crisscrossed the fat, white clouds. I told her what I'd told no one else—and she never flinched.

Instead, she held my hand, as if she would never let it go.

". . . so I guess you could say I remain pretty messed up. My folks worried I'd put a bullet through my head, and, well, I most likely would have, if something hadn't changed."

"Were you really afraid you'd actually do it?"

"What do you mean?"

"Were you really afraid you'd kill yourself?"

"Yeah, I've thought a lot about it. I was so tired. Tired of reliving the day Kev died. Tired of everybody tiptoeing around me. Before Kev died, everything was cool. I mean, we did all sorts of stuff. We had a blast and school was fun. Heck, Coach even said he wanted me to try out for quarterback, but that'll never happen now."

"Alex, it wasn't your fault."

"Huh? Weren't you listening? I'm lucky the cops believed. . . "

"Stop it! It wasn't your fault. You didn't kill Kevin!"

"Hey! I was there; I know what happened. If we hadn't been racing, he wouldn't be dead."

Rachel took my face in her hands.

"Alex, it was an accident. Yeah it was a stupid bet, but Kevin was having fun. He just didn't see the truck. You couldn't have done anything to stop it. It . . . it just happened. Life is like that. One minute you're here and the next you're not. Trust me, I know. Life is so hard. But no matter what anyone tells you, no matter what the kids whisper at school, Kevin's death was nothing more than a tragic accident."

I wanted to believe her, but some facts couldn't be explained away.

"What about his dad? What about that night at the hospital? What about what he said to me?" I shook my head. "He knew it was my fault. The police questioned me for weeks, and Bill and Clarise were still getting phone calls right before I came here."

"Alex, you have to realize that Kevin's father was in pain. The man had just lost a son. He lashed out. Think about how you feel right now and multiply that by a million. Kevin was his son, his only son. He was hurting. I'm sure he didn't mean what he said."

"You don't know. You weren't there; he was so mad." I stared at my feet. "No, he knew. He knew I'd killed Kev. I should have warned Kev about the truck. Mr. Rubenstein knew it was my fault. I should have stopped Kev that day. If I had, he'd be alive."

Rachel refused to believe me, but I knew it was only because she didn't have all the facts. I told her how everybody at school avoided me like I was contaminated, how I might as well have had "I killed my best friend" stamped on my forehead and been done with it. I told her about the nightmares. And the guilt.

Finally, it seemed like I'd convinced her.

She inched away from me. Her face grew cold. She gave her long hair a toss.

"So why did you do it?"

I cocked my head, not sure if I'd heard her right.

"What did you say?"

"Why did you do it?"

"What do you mean, 'why did I do it?'" I asked, my voice quavering.

"Well, if you killed Kevin, you must have had a reason. You know, a motive. So, why? I thought he was your best friend? Did you secretly hate him? Did he have something you wanted?"

She leaned closer to me and her eyes got large.

"Did you fight about another girl? Was it some secret blood fantasy? Why did you kill someone you say you loved so much?"

I drew back. This was messed up. She made me sound so cold-blooded.

"You've been watching too much CSI. I didn't say any of that. I didn't murder Kev."

Rachel smiled. "You didn't kill him, either."

And I realized she was right.

I hadn't killed Kev. The drunk driver had. I waited for the feelings of relief to come, for me to start feeling better. But nothing happened. My guts still ached. But then, Rachel wasn't finished with me just yet, either.

"Alex, stop being so macho for one moment. You didn't kill Kev, but you wouldn't be this messed up and hurt if you didn't love him. It's okay to admit that."

She sat up. She was so close the tips of our noses touched.

"Kevin was . . . your . . . best . . . friend. You had a bond as strong as the one brothers share. You loved him. It's okay to admit that. He sounds terrific."

I wasn't sure what to say next. I was still trying to deal with the realization that I was innocent in Kev's death. For so long I'd tried not to think about Kev. Instead I'd just stayed mad. I guess I was mad at him for dying and mad at myself because I couldn't stop it. I was mad at his dad and mad at Bill and Clarise and Jenny. I was even mad at God. More than anything, I missed Kev. I missed the jokes and the fun. I missed our stupid races. I missed hearing him laugh and hanging out at his house. I missed having him in my life. It had been almost a year since the accident, and just the thought of that day still made me want to puke.

Rachel didn't say anything for awhile. Instead, she nestled a little closer by my side. Then she leaned her head against my shoulder.

That's when I lost it. Tears welled up in my eyes. I knew they had been there all along, and now I couldn't stop them. I pulled my knees against my chest, ducked my head between them, and covered my ears with my arms so she wouldn't see me cry. For the first time since the night Kev died, I sobbed like a baby. Time stood still. Finally, I caught my breath. The sound of Rachel whispering my name broke through my anguish.

"Alex? Alex?"

"Yeah?"

"Are you okay? Is there anything I can do?"

I grabbed my shirt and made a lame attempt to dry my eyes.

"I'll be okay. It's just that everything still hurts so much."

"It's going to be okay. Sometimes crying helps."

"Not when you're a guy. You must think I'm a gutless coward."

"No."

I picked up a rock and gave it a heave. It bounced off the side of the cafeteria. "Your taste in guys isn't improving." I looked at Rachel, trying to read her. "Instead of some violent creep, now you're spending time with a sobbing, suicidal wuss."

Rachel gave me a look, like she saw right through me.

"I'll tell you what I think. I think you miss your best friend." Rachel wrapped her arms around me. She snuggled closer. "You wanna know something else?"

"I guess."

"I think Kevin sounds like a wonderful person. I wish I'd had the chance to know him."

I sucked the snot back down my throat and dried my eyes again. No more crying. Rachel took my hand.

"It sounds to me like you two made a great team. He was lucky he had a friend who cared about him so much. From what you've told me Kevin was your absolute, do-anything-for, happy-to-get-busted-with friend."

I looked into her face.

For the first time someone understood.

# CHAPTER TWELVE

R ACHEL AND I talked for a little while longer, but then it was time for me to head back to the cabin. Wah-Sha-She students had to report by four in the afternoon or the counselors went looking for them. Stay gone too long and the guards— then the police—came after you.

I made it with five minutes to spare.

"I was beginning to wonder about you." Rick eyed me cautiously, as if he wasn't sure just what I'd been up to. "Cutting it close. Don't you think?"

I pointed to the clock.

"I had five minutes to spare. I was with Rachel. Honest."

Rick smiled, pleased.

"Good. After our conversation I wasn't too sure about you. Didn't think you talked to anyone."

The smile caught me off guard. I looked down at my feet. I don't know, maybe I'd misjudged Rick. For several days, I'd overheard Lard Butt talking about how cool Rick was; how Rick cared about our troubles. I hadn't believed him, until I saw Rick smile just now. The smile, well, the smile looked real. He was actually happy I was with Rachel.

"Yeah," I said. "Rachel explained a lot to me . . . she's . . ."

Behind me, Lard Butt laughed.

"You were talking to Rachel?"

"Yeah."

Lard Butt plopped down on the floor in front of me. I noticed his clothes seemed loose on him.

"She's great," he said. "I met her at a scholastic meet last year. She was the one who told me about this place."

He patted his stomach.

"She said it could help me overcome my eating addiction. I'm glad I listened to her. She's pretty amazing. And, man is she beautiful." Lard Butt shook his head in amazement.

I couldn't disagree. "That she is."

"Alex you don't know the half of it," Rick said. "There's steel under all those curves."

He walked towards the door.

"Since all of you are all here and accounted for, I'm off to my next assignment. Remember lights out at eleven."

On his way out, Rick stopped by me.

"You know Alex, you should get to know your cabin mates—Gus, Trevor, and Jim Bob. I think you'd like them. They're good guys."

I thought Rick was yanking my chain.

Two days later, I realized he was telling the truth.


OKAY, SO I WAS WRONG. Real wrong. When I first met Lard Butt, Wheezer, and Hillbilly I wrote them off before exchanging a single word with them. But as the nights went by that summer and I listened to them talk to each other after lights-out, I realized Rick was right.

They were okay. That realization came to me one night in front of the TV, while my three roommates were sitting in front of the tube hanging out and talking. I was in my normal spot, by myself, across the room, with one ear bud plugged in, trying to read—and to ignore the three Musketeers.

"It was a pretty messed up time," I heard Wheezer telling the other two. "Dad lost his job, and then my uncle—his brother—died, and then we lost our house. Dad just snapped."

Wheezer stopped talking, but he had my attention.

He looked around, as if he was about to share a secret.

"That's . . . that's when everything happened."

"What do you mean?" Lard Butt said.

"My dad killed my mom," Wheezer said, quietly. "We were all asleep. Dad got up, poured gasoline all over the house, and lit it."

His voice broke.

"I . . . I smelled the smoke first. Cassie, my sister, and I got out, but Mom—she didn't make it."

I thought my life sucked. His story was no less intense—fire, death, and destruction. No wonder Trevor freaked out at school, got himself in trouble. One day he was just a kid. The next day he was an orphan. Bill and Clarise drove me nuts, but at least they liked each other. I thought about what had brought Trevor to Wha-Sha-She, maybe I'd been focused on my own problems for so long, I hadn't stopped to think about anyone else's.

LARD BUTT WAS FIGHTING his own battle. Yeah, he was big, but I had to admit he was waging a serious in-your-face war on his weight. His doctor had him working out twice a day, and he was only allowed to eat protein, fruits, and vegetables. And he was sticking with it.

I could tell he was serious about getting fit; I could see it in his face. I had been at the gym earlier in the week to work out, and, as always, he was there, too. I was in my usual dark mood, so I barely acknowledged him, but I couldn't help overhearing two guys next to me talking about how hard they'd seen Lard Butt working these past few weeks. Our paths crossed a couple more times at the gym, and one afternoon Lard Butt made a point of coming over to talk to me.

"You don't know what it's like, Alex," he told me. "I used to break out in a sweat just tying my shoes. People think if you're fat, you're stupid. They . . . they call you names."

I swallowed hard. For weeks I'd been calling him Lard Butt—and not just behind his back. It had never occurred to me that doing so might make life worse for a guy whose body already made him a target of snide remarks.

"Gus, I'm sorry, man," I said. "I was being a jerk. Sometimes I can be pretty stupid."

It would have served me right if he'd turn on his heels and left me standing there looking like a fool. But Gus was a better man than me.

He smiled and stuck out a huge paw.

"Yeah. But it's okay. I misjudged you, too. I didn't realize what you'd been through."

I rubbed my face, confused. "You mean you know?"

"Yeah, Rachel told me. It would suck to watch a friend die."

He had that right.

"Guess I'm not dealing with it too well."

Gus smiled. "You'll be okay. I can tell."

For some reason that made me smile. I'm not sure why, but knowing Gus thought I could make it, well, it meant something to me. It gave me hope.

"So how do you know Rachel?"

"Like I said, we're pretty good friends. She's the one who told me about this place. I would have liked to ask her out, but she was with Danny at the time. And, well, that was before I met Susan."

I did a double take.

"I didn't realize you had a girlfriend."

"Yeah, she's beautiful and funny, and, well, I'm pretty lucky."

Gus handed me his wallet. He showed me a photograph of a pretty girl with flaming red hair.

"Boy, you did good."

"That I did." Gus smiled. "She's another reason I'm here. I want to be around for a long, long time. I want to be with her forever, and I have to be healthy to do that. She's why I'm so focused."

"You're a machine," I said. "You're here every day. I've never seen anyone that focused."

Gus slapped me on the back and grinned, but I could tell he appreciated the compliment.

"Thanks man. I'm glad we understand each other."

He headed back to the weight machine. As he walked away, I thought: you gotta respect somebody who tries that hard.

AFTER THAT, GUS, TREVOR, and I became pretty good friends. I still didn't consider them run-of-the-mill guys, but I understood them. I recognized them for the originals they were, and they put up with all my weirdness. They reminded me that I wasn't the only one with problems in this world.

Hillbilly, now that was a different story.

Though he spent a lot of time with Gus and Trevor when I wasn't around, he never talked to me much. As someone who also appreciated his privacy, I was fine leaving him to his own little world. I did quit calling him Hillbilly, but, honestly, I don't know if he even noticed his nickname had been retired.

Maybe Rick saw something in him that I couldn't see, but I didn't sweat it. We were all getting along a lot better than before; no one said we had to be best buds. I decided it didn't matter if JimBob and I were friends.

But like so much in my life, that, too, soon changed.

# CHAPTER THIRTEEN

THE NEXT FEW weeks zipped by. Rachel and I started spending most of our time together. We talked at breakfast. We talked at lunch. We went for walks and talked late into the night. One night, we both snuck out of bed and met by the lake. That night, we also almost got caught. It was about two in the morning, and we were down by the boat dock. Rachel was snuggled up next to me, and we were gazing at the stars when I heard something.

"Hey, what was that?"

Rachel looked at me and shook her head.

"I don't know. What did you hear?"

"It sounded like someone whistling."

An off-key version of "Oh My Darling, Clementine" floated on the breeze. And it was getting louder.

"Come on."

I grabbed Rachel's hand, and we slipped around the back of the boat dock. We stood there for a few minutes. The whistling stopped. Then we quietly tiptoed back across camp to Rachel's cabin.

"Do you think we were seen?"

I shook my head. "Naw. We're okay."

We'd talked for hours, and now it was almost sunrise. I slipped into the woods and crept back to my cabin. I pushed the door open and cursed under my breath when it moaned, like a sick animal. I snuck inside and, quietly, crawled into bed. An hour later, I was up for breakfast. I found Rachel getting coffee in the cafeteria. She waved and pointed to an empty table near a window facing the lake.

"You don't look like someone who has been up all night," I said, as I pushed the sugar bowl towards her.

"Thanks!" Rachel said with a smile. "It's funny; I don't feel tired. It was a great talk. I had fun."

Just as I was about to agree, Rick came up and sat down at our table. He was wearing his "boy are you in trouble" look. "Alex, after breakfast I need to see you and Rachel. It's important."

The blood drained from my face. Rachel looked like she'd just been told the world had ended. "Ah, okay. Is something wrong?"

Rick looked at a knot hole in the table and drummed his fingers for a few seconds. Finally, he stopped and took a good hard look at each of us. "You could say that. We know you and Rachel snuck out of your cabins last night. That's a serious violation of the rules."

Rachel's face turned bright red.

"Rick, it's not like you think," Rachel said. "Honest. All we did was talk."

"You know, Rachel, you've never lied to me before. I hope that's the case now."

I sat my coffee down. I needed to make this right.

"Rick, please the fault is mine. I was the one . . ."

Rick waved me off, then stood and walked away.

"Save it for later, Alex. We'll talk then."

So much for my karma.

OK, YOU KNOW THOSE times that your parents tell you you're in big trouble and you freak about it? This was one of those times.

Only Rachel was the one who did the freaking. I guess she's never done a bad thing in her life, because for the next hour she ping-ponged between crying with worry and wanting to march over to Mr. Redding's office and smack him upside the head.

Right now she was crying.

"Alexxx . . . I . . . I don't know what I'll do if they call my parents; that would be horrible. It would be so embarrassing. If I get in trouble here, I might lose my chance of going to the academic meet."

I tried to reassure her. "Hey, they love you. You know that. I'm the one who asked you to come out after hours. I'm the one who should be in trouble. It's my fault, and I'll tell them that. I promise."

Rachel gave me a weak smile. "You're sweet, but nobody held a gun to my head and made me go. It was my own choice."

"Well, freaking out about it won't help, will it?"

Rachel nodded, reluctantly.

"I . . . I just really wanted to talk to you," she said. "I don't think that's so wrong."

WE SHOULD NEVER HAVE WORRIED. After an hour of chewing on me—first by Rick and then, Mr. Redding, they let me go. Rachel didn't even have to talk to Rick. She spent about ten minutes explaining to Mr. Redding, then walked out of his office with a huge smile.

"I shouldn't have worried," she said. "He said he wasn't happy that I snuck out, but he believed me, and, well, he even said he was glad you and I were spending so much time together. He said I'm good for you. But he also said if we did it again, they'd contact our parents and send us both home."

Not what I expected at all.

*Tonight on the "Alex Anderson Show," Alex breaks the rules, gets away with it, and still manages to have a de-*

*cent conversation with the girl. Tune in for highlights after
your local news.*

DON'T GET ME WRONG. I love spending time with Rachel.
We get along great, and I was pretty sure she saw me as possible
boyfriend material. What I wasn't sure about, was how I felt about
her. I mean I knew we were good friends, close friends, but I wasn't
sure if I wanted anything more. For a long time, I'd been the guy
at school who dated around. Even before the accident, I didn't get
close to anyone, and I never let anyone get close to me—except Kev.

Rachel was nice and sweet and funny, but I was still not back to
my old self. I wasn't sure I wanted a girlfriend. I wasn't sure it was
fair to a girl to try and be a boyfriend when I was still so screwed up
inside. And I was a little wary of her, too—partly because of the
strange connection we shared. It was like she could read my mind.
I would start thinking about everything that happened the day Kev
died, and I'd start to feeling guilty and Rachel wouldn't be anywhere
around then, bam! Next thing I knew, she was standing there, like
she'd been summoned.

And, okay, I was also having all sorts of wild dreams about her.
And even those were all twisted. I'd start to dream about her, but
before anything could happen between us, I'd flashback to the accident. In one dream I saw Rachel on my motorcycle. I walked towards her, and, as I reached out to touch her, I glanced down at my
hands—they were covered in blood.

Still as strange as everything remained as far as my days and my
nights, I couldn't stand not being around Rachel. The feelings were
almost too much for me to handle. Trust me, it isn't easy to hang
out with a girl—even one as great as Rachel—when twisted, graphic
images fill every corner and crevice of your mind.

But Rachel didn't give up.

That should have helped, but it didn't.

That's because I knew there was something else going on, something not with me but with Rachel. My gut told me she'd been either hurt or scared sometime in her past, or something terrible had happened to her, too.

I don't know how I knew—maybe it takes one to know one, but I was convinced this time *she* was hiding something, something *she* didn't want to talk to *me* about.

# CHAPTER FOURTEEN

THE DAY I LEARNED her secret Rachel was acting particularly strange. It was hot—one of those days in southeastern Oklahoma that makes you want to try and fry eggs on the sidewalk. Everybody had stripped down as far as they could without getting busted for indecent exposure. My afternoon pottery class was canceled because of a dead air conditioner in the education center. I started looking for shade. I hadn't gotten very far when I heard my name being called.

"Alex?" Gus stomped toward me. He'd lost more weight, which probably explained why his clothes didn't seem to fit quite right or to match—he looked like a lost tourist in white shorts, a lime green T-shirt, and neon-yellow sunglasses.

"Yeah?"

"Trevor, JimBob, and I want to go swimming. Ya wanna go?"

I was about to say not "no, but heck no," when another wave of sweat rolled down my back. It was so hot I had to agree that sitting in any water was better than trying to stay cool under the small withered, leafless tree I'd found.

"Yeah, I'll go. Let me change."

I stood up, ran inside, and slipped on my cutoffs.

"I have tons of sunscreen," Gus hollered from outside the cabin. "If ya wanna borrow some."

I grabbed a towel and vaulted over the porch rail. I landed behind Gus with a thump.

"Good idea. I may need some."

Gus laughed. "Gosh, Alex. You should run track or something."

We started for the lake. Most of our fellow campers were already there, but I didn't see Rachel. I hadn't seen her all day.

"Hey, Alex?"

"Yeah?"

"How are things with Rachel?"

He'd caught me by surprise. I still didn't think of Rachel as more than a friend. "Ahhh, okay. I guess."

Gus smiled; his face turning into one huge dimple with teeth.

"She's wonderful," he said. "You know she's not from around here, don't ya?"

"Yeah. She told me she's from Amarillo, Texas."

"She is mega smart. She kicked my butt at last year's academic meet." Gus leaned toward me and whispered. "I think she *really* likes you, too."

"Ahh, I don't know about that."

Gus rolled his eyes, while slathering a blob of sunscreen onto his arms.

"Well, she's, like, always talking to you. And you guys always eat together. I'd say she's laid claim to you."

Gus had nailed me again. Rachel had told me she liked me, but I didn't know about this *really* liking me business. Here, I had thought nobody had noticed us hanging out. Why am I always the last person to figure this stuff out?

Gus walked ahead of me. He'd caught on quick that I didn't want to talk anymore about Rachel. He didn't say anything else until we had almost reached the lake. Everywhere people splashed and dunked each other, acting stupid. Gus started waving his arms.

"There are JimBob and Trevor! Hey guys over here, I brought Alex. Come on Alex, let's hit the beach!" Gus bounced toward the water. "Yo! You coming?"

I swear I felt the earth move.

"Yeah. I'll be there in a minute."

I watched him tromp his way across the sand to the water. He sure seemed happy. I don't know how he did it, but in the short time we'd been here he'd made all sorts of friends.

I may have been the guy with the gym body and letter jacket, the guy the world would probably say had it all, and nothing could have been further from the truth. Gus, on the other hand, fought a weight problem while the whole world watched, and he had a million friends. I stood there, on the beach, alone, while he kicked back in the water with a dozen or so other morons—each and every one of them looking like they were having a blast.

*Today on the Teen Channel, psycho-basket case Alex Anderson tries to understand the rest of the world—not realizing he's the most screwed up one of all. Brought to you by parents everywhere.*

I STEPPED SLOWLY AROUND the people on the sand, certain Rachel was there somewhere. I looked by the slide, next to the concession stand, nothing. I kept walking and looking but no Rachel. I wiped the sweat out of my eyes. This heat could melt steel.

All around me people splashed and screamed. Guess I wasn't in the mood for swimming after all. I didn't care what everyone else was doing, I'd have preferred to be inside, by myself—anywhere than on a beach surrounded by a bunch of screaming idiots I didn't know. I was just about to act on that thought when a girl's voice distracted me.

"Hey Alex?"

I looked to my right. A thin girl on a huge, red beach towel—Aubrey Simpson—waved at me.

"Have you been in the water yet?"

I shook my head. "Just got here."

"Oh," Aubrey said.

No one has ever accused Aubrey of being a brain surgeon. Oh, she's okay, but in her own way she's weird, too. She is tall, with stringy brown hair and the laugh of a hyena; she also prays louder than anyone else. And I don't think she has ever missed a scheduled camp activity.

Aubrey tugged on my towel. "Are you looking for Rachel?"

"Huh?"

"Rachel? Are you looking for Rachel?"

What was this? Was the whole camp keeping tabs on us? It was probably in the camp newsletter or on the Internet at Alex-has-a-thing-for-Rachel-dot-com. Whatever.

"Well, yes, I guess."

"She's over there, by the north boat dock." Aubrey pointed to a rickety boat dock on the north side of the lake. "I think she was looking for you . . ."

I didn't hear the rest.

I was headed north.

# CHAPTER FIFTEEN

FOR THE RECORD, it's impossible for me to sneak up on Rachel. She must have some type of Alex ESP, or she's psychic, or something. Whatever it was, I could not surprise her. Believe me, I have tried. More than once.

This time I was about forty feet behind her, moving slowly and quietly. Rachel sat on the dock with her back to me. Her hair was pulled back, and she wore a long cotton T-shirt dress, thin enough to be interesting but covering what needed to be covered.

Through the material, I saw the faint outline of a skimpy blue-and-yellow bikini. I walked quietly towards her, had just taken my third to the last step, and . . .

"I take it you've been looking for me?"

So much for the surprise attack.

"Man, Rachel, you must have super human hearing. I swear you could hear a mouse in soggy tennis shoes crawling across a damp rag."

She laughed. "Well, I know I have good hearing, but it's never been described like that before."

I stepped on the dock and dropped down beside her.

"You gotta forgive me. Every now and then I use Kev-speak."

"Ohhh," she said.

I pointed to the water. "So why are you sitting here alone? Aren't you the chief Get Happy Person of Girls Cabin 1?"

Rachel turned and gave me a look that said, "I may think you're great, but don't push your luck."

"I'm not alone." She waved her hand in a lazy circle. "There are people everywhere."

"Bull. You're half a football field away, sitting by yourself on a beat-up old boat dock. Why?"

"I'm . . . I'm not much for swimming."

"I thought you liked to swim?"

"Well, I do. But I'm not very good at it."

Now it was my turn to laugh, I pointed to the other beach.

"If you wanna see 'not good' go watch Gus. Seriously, it's like watching the Titanic sink all over again."

Rachel tried not to giggle, but she couldn't help herself.

"Alex! You shouldn't say things like that. That's not very nice."

"Hey, those are Gus's own words," I said. "Besides, you haven't seen him swim."

'It's still not nice."

"Okay, okay, sorry. You're right, Gus is a good guy and he's my friend." I tugged on her arm.

"Lose the T-shirt and let's hit the water."

Rachel shook her head.

"I told you I'm not very good."

"That's okay. I'm Red Cross-certified. I promise you won't drown. I'll teach you."

She gave me a weak smile.

"Alex, I'd rather not. I mean I'm just not . . ."

I stood and backed away from her about ten feet.

"Come on. It's too hot not to try."

She started to complain, and I started to run. I made a wild dash to the end of the dock and leapt in the air. Right before I hit the water I grabbed my knees. The cannonball soaked her. Rachel stood and shook like a wet poodle.

"Alex, you are rotten! Look at me. Now I'm all wet!"

"Yeah? So? What's the big deal?"

I reached up and tried to pull her into the water.

"Come on. I promise I won't let you sink."

"You swear?"

I held up three fingers—the official Boy Scout salute.

"I swear."

Rachel slipped into the water. At first she seemed scared, then she started to enjoy herself. She kept her T-shirt on.

I cocked my head, looking at her suspiciously.

"You *really* don't know how to swim?"

She splashed me. "Well, I could probably dog paddle a fair distance, but, honestly, I'm not any good."

I slipped my arm around her waist and pulled her towards me.

"I could teach you, if you want."

She smiled. I watched small beads of water drip from her hair, then slide down her long, slender neck.

"That would probably be . . . fun."

I splashed her again.

"Great! The Alex Anderson School of Swimming is now open. All students report to the teacher."

Rachel paddled away from me and smiled.

"So, what do we do first?" she asked.

"That's easy." I reached for her T-shirt. "First you need to lose this. It's too big and bulky—it'd be like trying to swim with an anchor around your neck."

I started to tug the wet T-shirt over her head, but Rachel turned and, with the speed of a cheetah, slapped my hand away.

"No. Stop that!" Her face was tense, almost angry.

"Relax I wasn't being fresh or anything."

She glared at me, like she was ready for a fight.

"I know that!" Rachel said. "I didn't think you were! Just leave my shirt alone. Okay?"

I held my hands up and kicked away.

"Okay, sorry."

Rachel looked at me, then just as quickly, her face went soft and gentle again.

"I didn't mean to bite your head off. It's just I'm sensitive about this bikini. I don't want everyone looking, okay?"

"Well, okay. But why wear it if you don't want people looking?"

The reasoning of women—young or old—never failed to confound me. Rachel splashed her way to me and took my hand.

"You don't understand. I don't want, well, I don't want *everybody* looking."

I rolled my eyes. "Well, the rest of the frigging camp is two blocks away. And besides, I'm not just anyone, am I? I thought you and I were, well, I thought we were . . ."

"We are, silly," Rachel said. "You're special to me, too. I guess I'm a little modest. Okay?"

Since I had no intention of starting a fight over wearing or not wearing a T-shirt, I nodded. Rachel smiled and paddled closer.

"Now, I thought you were going to teach me how to swim."

I took her in my arms, and we splashed and played for awhile, but I could tell she wasn't having a good time. She was distracted. Something was wrong. I wasn't sure what to think, but I knew that stuff about not wanting to be seen in her bikini was a lie.

I think this time she was the one keeping the secret.

# CHAPTER SIXTEEN

TRY KICKING faster." I put my hand in the small of her back and pushed up to keep her from sinking. She kicked her legs back and forth.

"Like that?" Rachel asked as she sank from view.

I smiled. Rachel was right. She was no swimmer.

"Well, not bad." I said as I pushed her back up and to the surface. Rachel flipped out of my hands and faced me.

"I told you I wasn't very good. I like to splash in the water, but I, well, I just don't swim well."

"Yeah, I believe you." I said, with a grin.

WE SWAM AND PLAYED a little while longer, until Rachel took off paddling to the dock. I tried to help her out, but she batted my hand away again.

"Don't!" she said. "I can do it myself."

"Sorry, just trying to help."

I looked at her face. Today's Rachel was not the Rachel I was used to hanging out with. I felt like I had done something wrong. Rachel crossed her legs and pulled her hair back from her face. She looked at me and smiled.

"What's wrong?" she asked.

"Nothing. I'm fine."

"Are you mad at me?"

I gave her my patented, "you must be nuts" look.

"Who said anything about being mad?" I said. "Me? I'm not mad. Why would I be mad? What would I have to be mad about? I am the exact opposite of mad. Everything's fine."

Rachel looked doubtful.

"You know, Alex, you don't lie very well. Your face says it all. So I can only assume you're upset about something."

Now it was my turn to glare at her.

"Do you ever stop analyzing people? You are constantly trying to figure me out."

"Well, I think you're worth the effort. You still haven't answered my question. Are you *mad* at *me*?"

I knew when I was nailed. The smart response would be to get it out and over with. I gritted my teeth and pulled myself up and out of the water and next to her on the dock.

"Well, yeah, a little. But not that much."

Rachel looked confused.

"Keep talking, I'm not sure I follow."

"It's just that it's like you're two different people," I said. "The other day you were all sweet and stuff, but today the second I try to help you out of the water, you slap my hand. Jeez, I feel like a little kid being punished."

Rachel stared at her toes, wiggled them, and finally spoke.

"I didn't mean it like that, I'm sorry, Alex. It's . . ."

I held up a hand to stop her. I needed to finish what I had to say.

"It's like now you're the one hiding stuff," I said. "You made me tell you everything—all my problems—everything. You know stuff about me that Bill and Clarise don't know, that nobody else knows.

But today, when I tried to talk to you, you act as if I've done something wrong. And Rachel, this time it's *you* who hasn't said what's bothering you.

"So what gives? I don't understand. Why do I have to spill my guts to you, but you don't have to do the same? It seems . . . kind of two-faced, ya' know?"

Rachel ran her hands through her hair, like a girl on a music video, then brought her face up to mine—slowly.

"You're . . . you're right. I should tell you, it's just not easy for me to talk about it."

"I know the feeling. Remember our little discussion from a couple weeks ago? That wasn't easy for me either."

She smiled.

"Okay. Okay, you're right. That's why I came over here . . . I didn't want anyone else around. There's a lot to . . . explain."

"Fine, start explaining."

"I promise. How about tonight? After vespers?"

"Oh yeah, vespers. Wouldn't wanna miss that. How about now?"

Rachel slugged my arm.

"Alex!"

I took her hand and looked her straight in the eyes—turnaround was only fair. "I'm not letting you go, Rachel, until you tell me what's going on."


I COULD TELL BY THE expression on her face that Rachel felt cornered. And hearing her own words used against her, well, I guess she saw the irony in that. She bit her lip then looked at her hands.

"It's difficult to talk about. I'm not sure where to start."

I could tell she was struggling with how and where to begin.

"How about the beginning?" I suggested. "Why don't you start there."

Rachel looked at me confused. "What do you mean?"

"Why don't you tell me the real reason you're here." I waved my arms in a big circle. "You know why Gus is here. You know why I'm here. You know why Trevor is here. But you're not like any of us. You're beautiful and normal and sane. So why are you here?"

"Are you sure you want to know?"

"Yeah, I am."

Rachel stood and turned away from me. In one, swift motion she peeled off her T-shirt and tossed it on the dock. For a moment, she hesitated, frozen in place with her back to me.

"Are you sure you want to know? You can still back out."

Her actions had startled me and the fear in her voice scared me, but I knew she had a reason for tearing off the T-shirt she'd been so desperate to hold onto just minutes ago in the water.

"Hey, it can't be that bad," I said, reaching for her.

Slowly, she turned towards me.

"This . . . this is why I'm here."

At first I didn't see anything but a beautiful girl in a bikini, then I looked at her face. Tears drifted down her cheeks.

"I don't understand," I said. "What do you mean?"

She pointed to the valley formed by her bathing suit top. There, a thin jagged line ran from between her breasts down her belly. Right above her belly button, the line stopped in a tiny swirl.

"What happened?"

Rachel sat down. She looked out over the lake.

"This is why I'm here. I had surgery and spent a long time in the hospital. My doctor thought it would be a good idea for me to get some sun and be outside."

I looked at the long, thin scar. One of the guys on my football team had had knee surgery last year. I remembered him showing everyone his scar, but it was nothing compared to this. This was like someone had taken a portrait of a beautiful woman and cut a thin jagged line down it. I reached for Rachel's hand.

"What type of surgery was it? What was wrong?"

"I had heart surgery. I was really sick," Rachel said. "I almost died."

Now that I had my answer, I wasn't sure what to do with it. I wanted to say something comforting, something that wouldn't come off stupid, but I wasn't sure what that was.

"I'm . . . I'm sorry," I said. "Now I understand why you didn't want to take the T-shirt off. I didn't know."

Rachel leaned her head on my shoulder.

"It's okay. I would love to learn how to swim, but I hate looking at myself in the mirror. I'm like Frankenstein. I'm hideous. I've been all cut up and stitched back together. It's gross."

"I never said that."

"Huh?"

I reached up, cupped her chin, and turned her face towards me.

"I said, 'I never said that.' I don't think you're hideous. I think you're beautiful. And amazing."

"But I thought."

"You thought what? Heck, Rachel, I know I'm insane and weird and shallow, but I'm not blind. I know a beautiful girl when I see one."

Rachel gave me a faint smile.

"You mean you don't mind? Even with the scar?"

Softly, I traced the thin scar.

"No . . . no I don't. I've never met anyone like you. When I'm around you I feel good. And everything is better with you. I haven't felt that way in a long, long time. I could care less if you have a scar. Okay?"

Rachel sniffled, then wiped her eyes.

"Alex, I just . . . I really like you and . . . "

"Shhhh," I said, then I leaned in and kissed her.

Her lips were full and soft.

"I think you're beautiful. Scar and all."

# CHAPTER SEVENTEEN

IT WASN'T EASY trying to sleep with Trevor in the top bunk. He wheezed loudly. My ninety-year-old granny breathes better than he did. It was the same every night: Trevor climbed into the bunk above me, then hung over the side to talk. We'd talk for a while, then I'd listen to him try to breath for the rest of the night.

"So, ahhhhh, Alex . . . " *Actually, Trevor didn't talk. He spewed words in between gasps for air.* "Whaaat . . . ahhhhhh brought you to . . . ahh-hhhh camp Wah-Sha-She?"

I rubbed my eyes, faked a yawn, and stretched.

"My folks made me."

"Really? Me, too! Ahhhhhh . . . me too! Are you staying until August?" he asked.

"Yeah."

"Well, that's . . ." Trevor paused mid-sentence to hack up something plugging his lungs. Ten minutes later he was ready to talk again. Me, not so much.

"Listen Trevor, if ya don't mind, I'd like to get some sleep."

"Oh . . . sure."

I heard him roll over. I listened to him wheeze and cough for a few minutes, and after another few minutes he turned his bunk light off. Outside the crickets chirped. Somewhere out in the woods the hoot of an owl reminded me what it was like to be lonely. He could have spared the effort. I understood lonely just fine.

I WASN'T SURE HOW LONG I slept, but it wasn't long enough. Trevor was sleeping the sleep of the dead. Funny, he breathed normally when he was deeply asleep. It was only when he was awake that he sounded like a freight train with a head cold.

I jerked awake, as if I'd been jolted with electricity.

Snakes twisted and turned in my gut. Suddenly I was scared, so scared my hands trembled. I chewed on my lower lip. Sweat dripped down my back. I looked around the room. In the gray light, I saw Gus splayed across his bed. A few feet over, JimBob sighed quietly, then rolled onto his back. JimBob slept like a baby. Must be nice.

I drummed my fingers on my bed frame. The air was sticky. I would have killed for some central air-conditioning instead of our rusty ceiling fan that struggled to turn four blades. I wiped the sweat out of my eyes. Enough of this. Time for some fresh air. I slipped out of bed and crept toward the door. After two tries with the lock, I stood on the porch—and the snakes in my gut started slam dancing.

A FULL MOON GLOWED through the branches of an old, twisted walnut tree. A few feet away the cicadas droned, with the sound of a dying electric motor. Such nights always reminded me of Kev. We used to sit in his backyard and eyeball the moon through his high powered telescope.

"That's the Sea of Tranquility." Kev would say, pointing to the spot on the moon where Apollo 11 landed in 1969 and Neil Armstrong became the first man to walk on the moon. "And over there, that bright star is Mars, the red planet."

Funny, I used to like to look at the moon. I knew the constellations. I could point out the Milky Way. Now I barely bothered to look up, no matter how clear the night sky. I sat down on the porch rail. The breeze felt cool against the dampness of my shirt. In the distance thunder rumbled. In my belly, the snakes danced.

TWELVE-THIRTY. I'D DOZED off. I was still on the porch, a marching band doing a halftime show inside my chest. I'd probably caught whatever Trevor had hacked up. Just what I needed, the Black Crud. I stood and stretched. The darkness was thick, like a blanket. The air still. My heart thumped. I must be screwed up. I was scared and I didn't know why. *So this was how a frog in a blender felt.*

In front of me, a tall pine tree swayed in the breeze. The wind in the branches made a sad moan—like an ill child. In the distance, the thunder rolled. A storm moved towards camp. The air bristled with electricity. Everything felt strange. I had hoped being outside would clear my head, but inside my gut was a feeling I couldn't shake, the feeling that somewhere, something was wrong.

I walked to the far end of the boys' side of camp. Beyond was a path that led east, a short hike back to the Great Hall. That was one of the camp's few nice features: it didn't take long to get from the farthest cabin to the cafeteria. Since I had nothing better to do, that's where I headed. The night was still—no breeze, no owl, and no crickets—just a creepy silence.

A circle of dingy, yellow light and two, rusty steel barrels told me when I'd made it to the cafeteria's back entrance. My chest thumped like a drum. My hands trembled. I stepped into the shadows and took a deep breath. The snakes in my gut moved. My stomach felt full of acid. I puked on my shoes.

JUST BEYOND THE CAFETERIA, I saw the girls cabins. They were all dark. No one awake there. Rachel was in cabin one at the far end. She was probably crashed. We'd spent the whole afternoon in a canoe—me talking, her paddling. It was supposed to have been the other way around.

Nonetheless, it had been a good afternoon. And, yeah, I missed her. I figured it would help to talk to her. She'd understand. I wondered for a moment if she'd get mad if I woke her up? The girls cabins were slightly larger than ours. But right now only four of them were being used. The two cabins in the middle were vacant.

I walked towards cabin one, trying to stay in the shadows. If I got caught, there would be, at the least, a call home to Bill and Clarice, and at worst, a swift kick out the door. Mr. Redding might act like someone who wanted to be your friend, but he was strict when it came to enforcing camp rules. He wouldn't be looking to do me any favors either, especially since I already had a record.

I kept walking. I tried to be quiet, like Kev had taught me. He called this "shadow walking," said his grandpa had taught him how to do it. He had all kinds of stories about how his granddad could creep up on anyone. "It's all in the way you step," he would say. "You can't just go stomping along. You gotta move swiftly and lightly, like a fox."

Yeah, right. Well, I was no fox. But I was also no bulldozer. And, just so you know, Trevor sleeping made more noise than I did in the great outdoors. Anyway, I'd made it to Girls Cabin 3, when the first drops of rain started.

I looked at the sky. It was probably going to rain all night. By morning the place would be a mud puddle again. It was hard to remember the last time I had had dry socks. Cabin three was one of the two cabins not being used, and it looked like it, too.

The boys cabins might have been old, but at least they've also been painted. Cabin three looked as if somebody pulled it out of the dumpster and plopped it on the ground, then walked away.

The rain cut loose, falling in sheets. I jumped the cabin's broken rail and crouched down on the porch. The air felt cool, but my stomach was a lava slide. I was sure I'd contracted some fatal intestinal disease. I tried to imagine myself as a slobbering, scab-covered monster.

I found a dry spot on the porch and wedged myself into the corner. I looked around. I understood why the cabin was being repaired. It creaked and moaned something awful. The windows were boarded, and the wood was either rotten or splintered. I figured the place could cave in any minute. I hoped Bill and Clarise hadn't paid too much to send me to this rat hole.

"Boom!" The sky rumbled.

Mother Nature was, officially, ticked off. Every few seconds thunder exploded. What a great time for a walk. Crash! A bolt of lightning sliced through the sky. The wind blew rain in my face. I was soaked. It was time to get inside. I'd dinked around on the porch and hadn't bothered yet to look around. What I saw now didn't look right. The front door was smashed in, as if someone had taken an ax and hacked his way through to the inside. There was a huge, splintered hole where the door knob used to be. One hinge was twisted and bent; the other hinge was gone.

I stepped inside and looked around. There, on the opposite wall, someone had smeared a muddy handprint.

The mud was still wet.

## CHAPTER EIGHTEEN

THE CABIN WAS dark, damp, and smelled stale. Built like all the others, it had two square bathrooms in the center jutting from the wall. The bunk beds sat at either end. My eyes adjusted to the dark quickly, and I spotted a dim light coming from the back of the cabin.

Both bathroom doors were open. Through them, I saw a faint, green glow. Trash and broken boards littered the place. I'd seen cleaner garbage cans. The biting, stale aroma of wet mattresses and urine hung in the air, like a toxic fog.

I took another step, stopped. I had a weird thought: I hoped Redding and the rest of the camp morons wouldn't think I'd kicked in that door. *When had I started worrying about what they thought?* I shrugged off the worry and walked towards the light, when I heard a strange sound.

"Ummmpth . . . Oh, plea . . ."

What the heck? It sounded a little like a voice, but it was difficult to tell with all the noise coming from the storm.

"Ummmpth!"

In my gut the snakes turned somersaults. I felt uneasy, scared. Something was nearby and hurt—probably a wild animal trying to avoid the wind and rain.

"Ummmpth . . . no, please . . ."

Now I knew something was wrong—really, friggin' wrong—animals didn't talk.

I crept towards the back of the cabin. My view was still obstructed. The rain bounced on the roof, like marbles falling in a tin can.

"Ohhhh please! No!"

That was definitely a voice. It sounded female.

I stopped, strained to listen, and heard someone harshly whisper "Shut up!"

Okay. Someone besides me was in the cabin.

"Oh . . . please . . . please!"

The voice sounded scared to death. I stood between the wall and the bathroom door and peeked through the space left between the hinges into the room. On the floor I saw two people. The taller one was bent over a squirming smaller figure.

"Hold still!"

"Please Danny, no! Please!"

This time the words were clear and strong.

Danny? Danny? That could mean only one thing: The girl on the floor was Rachel.

# CHAPTER NINETEEN

**M**Y GUTS WERE NOW IN my mouth. Just a few feet away, on the filthy floor of the first bathroom, Rachel was pinned on the floor in the dust and grime. In the dim light Snake Face raised his hand. Whaaam! The sound of the strike echoed in my ears. He leaned into Rachel's face.

"I said 'shut up!' "

He slapped her a second time, while he clasped Rachel's hands over her head. She was as trapped as any animal in a cage, but Rachel kept fighting—twisting and turning, trying to shake him off or to break his grasp, but with no hands to use, she was fighting a losing battle.

Danny pushed her shirt up with his free hand. I started to panic. I had to do something. I couldn't stand there and watch him rape Rachel. I went cold. What if he had a knife or a gun? What if he hurt Rachel? That thought hit me with the force of a jackhammer.

"Stop it, Danny!" Rachel screamed again. "Let me go!"

Danny snorted. He sounded raw, like a wild pig.

"I told you to 'shut up.' You yell again, and I'll really hurt you."

I stepped from behind the door and, softly, pulled it back a few more inches. I could see Danny's back. He was on his knees, on top of Rachel. Sweat soaked my shirt. I struggled to breathe. I slipped through the door and tiptoed towards them.

Rachel couldn't see me, but I now had a clear view as she struggled against Danny.

"Get off me! You're ripping my clothes. Get off!"

Rachel thrashed left and right. Danny slapped her again.

"See what you made me do? Just shut up! Okay? Do you want me to hurt you?"

"Wow, that's ugly." He was looking at the scar on her chest now. Rachel grimaced and closed her eyes, but not before I glimpsed the hopelessness in them. *Don't stop fighting now Rachel.*

"Please! No! Please, Danny. If you stop now, I promise I won't say anything to anyone, okay?"

Only a few seconds had passed since I recognized the two of them on the floor, but it felt like a lifetime. I needed a weapon, and I needed it now. I took three more steps. There, on the floor, by an old toilet I saw a two-by-four. It was about three feet long and solid cedar. Perfect.

Two more steps. I was breathing so loud now I didn't know how Danny didn't hear me. But Rachel was yelling. She hadn't seen me yet either.

Another step. A bolt of lightning struck outside. Man, was it loud! If Danny turned around at the wrong moment, my stealth attack would be ruined, and I'd be facing off with the guy one on one. Rachel tried again to free her hands. In the dim light I saw her eyes were wild with panic. Blood trickled down her face. I side-stepped to the left, to the edge of the shower, ready to strike.

She saw me now! I was sure of it. I looked at her again. Yes, she'd seen me—I could see it in her eyes. I put my finger to my lips, signaling her to stay quiet. The most imperceptible of nods, as she suddenly went limp. Her lips moved silently. I was pretty sure she was praying.

As Danny went to grope her again, I stepped directly behind him. He had both of his knees pinned against Rachel's shoulders and, luckily for me, one of his hands was busy keeping her hands at bay.

"Now let's get these off. . ." He reached back for the zipper on her shorts, putting himself in an awkward position.

He shouldn't have done that.

It cost him, big time.

I SWUNG HARD, as hard as I've ever swung a bat. I don't know where the power came from—rage, fear, insanity. The snakes in my gut all screamed in unison as wood hit flesh.

Thwack! The bat caught Danny just below his right shoulder and knocked him off Rachel, up against the wall. He screamed in pain. I swung again. This time I hit his arm. Bones crunched. Blood splattered my shirt. I tossed the beam aside and launched myself at him, wrapping both arms around his head and driving him, hard, into the wall. His face cracked the bathroom tile, more blood. We rolled across the floor—Danny kicking and throwing blind punches, while I managed three quick jabs to the face, one to his balls.

"Ouchhh!"

Danny rolled into a ball, grabbed his crotch, and moaned.

Rachel scooted away from him. She was hysterical.

I felt something damp on the right side of my face. I tasted blood. He must have landed a punch.

Danny got back up.

I WANTED TO KILL HIM—right there, right then in the cabin. Every time I thought of him on top of her, groping her, slapping her, threatening her, I hit him—as hard as I could. Each time he moved or tried to defend himself, I hit him. I wanted him dead. I wanted to rip him apart.

"So how does it feel now that you're the one being punched?" I shoved him against the wall. "I swear that's the last time you ever touch her!"

Danny kneed me in the balls. I sucked wind and fell backwards. He struggled to his feet and threw a wobbly, blind punch. Missed and lost his balance. He staggered a step and slid to the floor. Blood, like an angry red slash of paint, smeared the floor tile.

I grabbed another board and moved towards him.

This was it. This was my chance to get rid of the devil. This was my chance to even the odds. This was payback for Kev's death. This would quiet the snakes for good. I raised the board over my head and swung it full force at Danny's raw, bloody face.

"Whaaam!"

The board smashed into the wall, I'd missed Danny's head by inches. Splinters of wood and chips of tile filled the air. I turned to swing again. Danny rolled his head back and tried to cover his face. This time I wouldn't miss. This time I'd crush his skull.

This time—the board halted in mid-air.

"No! Alex. Please, no!" Rachel had grabbed my arm. "Don't be like him. Please?"

Her face was bloody and swollen and dirty, but her eyes shined. She tightened her grip on my arm. Slowly, I lowered the board. I was stunned. I didn't know what to do. I looked into her eyes for answers. Tears rolled down her cheeks.

I could feel her fighting for my soul.

"Please . . . Alex."

In the corner Danny moaned again. He had curled into a protective ball, like a rolypolly. He didn't look so scary now.

Rachel took my chin and turned my face to hers.

"Let it go. It's over. I'm okay. Let . . . it . . . go . . ." She sounded like Trevor—all raggedy breaths and nasty gasps.

I hugged her to me.

"Are you okay? You sound horrible."

I'm . . . I'm . . . fine," she said, between gulps of air. "Just . . .

need to . . . catch . . . my . . . breath . . . give me a sec."

I knew I would have waited for her much longer than that.



IT SEEMED LIKE hours later—it was actually only a few minutes—when Rachel pulled herself away from me and walked over
to the bloody mound that was Danny. She took a torn piece of her
shirt and wiped the blood off his face. Then she leaned over and
whispered in his ear.

"If I didn't hate violence so much I would have let him kill you,"
she said through clenched teeth. "I would have helped him, because
I have the right after what you've done to me. But revenge is never
the answer. All it would do is complicate and change my life and
who I am, and I'm not going to give you that kind of power.

"So consider yourself lucky, Danny—very, very lucky."

Rachel stood and walked away. I dropped the bloody board on
the floor. In the distance, the thunder rumbled.

# CHAPTER TWENTY

I FELL TO THE FLOOR exhausted and opened my eyes to find Rachel nowhere in sight. Blood covered my clothes. I called out for Rachel—but there was no response, nothing—just the sound of my ragged breathing and the moans of a would-be rapist.

"Rachel? Where are you?"

Behind me, Danny had come back to life. He snarled.

"I didn't do nothing," he said, in a broken lisp (*the fight appeared to have cost him a tooth or two*). "I'll have you hauled to jail!"

He stood, too dumb to know when to cut his losses. "She wanted to come here! She came with me!"

I headed for the front door. Maybe Rachel was outside. She wasn't. Where was she? The snakes in my gut began to move.

"Rachel? Where are you?"

"Alex?"

I couldn't tell if it was the rain talking or the wishful thinking of my screwed-up brain. Then I heard the voice again.

"Alex?"

It was only a faint whisper coming, from my right, from the corner by the front door. I walked towards it. Close to the floor, where both walls met, I saw a lumpy shadow.

"Rachel?"

She had folded herself into the fetal position, like she was still in the womb. Her arms hugged her knees. Her clothes were ripped to hell. Streaks of blood appeared here and there on the floor beside her. Her eyes were huge and glassy.

"Alex?" she whispered.

I knelt next to her on the floor.

"Are you okay, Rachel?"

Slowly, like fog lifting on a morning highway, the rest of Rachel's face came into focus. Long, dark veins lined her red cheeks. Near her left eye an ugly, purple bruise was rising on her skin. Her wrists were ringed with what could have been mistaken for a wristband tattoo but I knew were marks left by Danny's grip. She looked like I used to after going a few rounds with some of Stillwater's finer brawlers.

"Thought you'd bailed on me."

She whimpered, shaking her head "no."

"Can you stand?" I held out an arm to help her stand. She jerked away, and curled herself tighter into a ball. "Rachel...you're safe now. I promise."

Gently I pulled her to me.

She hesitated at my touch, but this time she didn't pull away.

"Alex it was . . ."

"I know I saw." I took her carefully in my arms. "It's okay; I'm here now. I'm sorry I wasn't here sooner. I'd have stopped him. I'm so sorry I didn't get here faster."

"It's okay." Rachel gave me a look like she'd never seen me before. "How did you figure out I was here?"

"I didn't."

She took a deep, ragged breath. Her hands shook as she wiped her face clean. She looked puzzled. She was about to say something to me then seemed to have second thoughts. "Then how'd you?"

I shook my head, knowing I probably looked as clueless as I felt.

"I was out for a walk and the rain started. I jumped on the porch to get out of it. The door was busted open. I came in and, well, found you two."

I skipped the part about the snakes and the feeling in my gut. She didn't need to know how mental I really was.

Rachel took my hand.

"If you hadn't come when you did, he . . . he would have." She started to cry, big heaving sobs.

"Rachel, I swear. If I'd known sooner, I would have . . ."

Before I could finish my sentence, Danny exploded. I'd forgotten he was even there. "If you'd just left us alone, we'd have been fine! Tell him Rachel. Tell him how you asked me here! Tell him the truth—you wanted it!"

Rachel's eyes flashed back and forth, from him to me.

"He's lying Alex! He told me he needed to talk, that something horrible had happened."

"It's okay, Rachel. I believe you. Okay?"

She smiled—only to have Danny lunge at her.

"I'm going to kill you!" He screamed and reached for Rachel with a bloody hand. I stepped sideways and shoved him out the front door. He tumbled outside and rolled off the porch. I pushed Rachel behind me, then stepped through the door.

"If you ever touch her again I *will* kill you," I said. "If you so much as call her I will find you."

Danny snarled. "Is that a threat, Mr. Psycho?"

I stepped forward. "No, a promise."

I'm not sure why, and to this day I still can't explain it, but Danny actually looked scared as I finished. He turned and screamed something about Clarise's morals. Then he stepped into the dark and disappeared.


RACHEL CLUNG TO ME. Her breathing ragged, as if she was

about to pass out. I noticed her shirt was in shreds and all but gone. Her shorts were torn and dirty. She was close to naked.

"Is he?"

I nodded.

"Yeah, he's gone. He just ran off, but something tells me he won't get far." I touched her shoulder. "It's okay. You're safe now. Here, you might need this."

I took my shirt off and handed it to her.

"Huh?"

"Your top's almost gone. I can see . . ."

"Oh!" Rachel blushed. She turned her back to me and started to slip into my shirt. Bruised and cut, she moved slowly. I turned away.

"Tell me when you're done, okay?"

I could hear her struggle with the shirt. She cried out from the pain. Tried again, and moaned from the effort.

"Alex, you're going to have to help me. I can't do this by myself. It hurts too much. Please?"

I turned back, and she handed me the T-shirt. I gently pulled it over her head. Her skin was pale and cold.

"Okay. Now, move your arm. There, we got it."

I unrolled the shirt over her belly. Rachel winced as the fabric hit her skin.

"Ouch, go slow, that hurts."

Another bolt of lighting slashed through the sky. For a second, the room was full of light, as surely as if someone had flipped a light switch on.

And for the second time I saw her scar.

I wanted to say something to her. I wanted to tell her that I cared. But for some reason I couldn't. What was wrong with me? She'd almost been raped. What was I thinking? This wasn't the time. Mentally, I gave myself a hard kick. Thank goodness my brain engaged before I said or did anything stupid.

I pulled her against me—trying not to cause her any more pain. She gave me a weak smile.

I smiled back. "You okay?" I asked.

"Yeah. Your shirt fits."

"Well, you couldn't run around in that other one. It just wasn't your color."

We walked out onto the porch. If I had thought we were in the clear, I was wrong. At the first touch of fresh air, her face crumpled. She covered her eyes with her hands and started to sob. When she spoke, the fear was back in her voice.

"Oh god, Alex. If you hadn't come, he . . . he would have . . ."

It was too awful to say out loud. She couldn't bring herself to finish the sentence. I put my arms carefully around her and began rocking her back and forth, like I was calming a frightened child.

> *. . . And yes, ladies and gentlemen, for the first time in a year, Alex Anderson has done something right. Stay tuned to see if he survives this test on "Survivor, The Alex Anderson Edition."*

# CHAPTER TWENTY-ONE

RACHEL AND I were in trouble. Deep trouble. Once the police found out about the attack, the news would get out—and the gossip would begin. The world as she knew it would for all practical purposes end for a girl who deserved a helluva lot better. I knew this from what had happened to me after Kev's accident. I hadn't deserved the wagging tongues either. And I'd be damned if I would let the gossips hurt Rachel like they had hurt me.

It was time to focus, but in my gut, the snakes slithered.

*They'll probably arrest me for . . . Stop it!* I needed to focus on Rachel and what she needed now; I could worry later about how I'd gone from being mad about Kev dying yesterday to almost killing a guy tonight.

"Rachel? We are in trouble. We have to get help. We have to tell somebody what happened."

Rachel moved closer to me. Her breathing was still ragged, but at least she'd stopped crying.

"What should we do?" she asked. "Should we see if we can find Danny and make sure that he's okay?"

I couldn't believe I had heard her right: Rachel wanted me to go make sure the guy who just tried to rape her was okay. Even Mother Teresa wouldn't have done that.

"Oh sure, why don't we water Hitler's flowers while we're at it?"

Rachel frowned. She didn't get the joke.

"Alex! Please?"

"Rachel, we have more important things to worry about than whether Danny needs some aspirin. We have to report this. I mean, jeez, a guy just tried to rape you. Remember."

Rachel's face twisted with fright. I wasn't sure what I'd said to warrant such a look.

"No! Oh no! Mr. Redding will call the cops! And my parents! There'll be an investigation! It will be all over camp. And you remember what Mr. Redding said last time. You and I will be sent home. Oh, Alex, you could get into so much trouble."

Her eyes welled with tears.

"I don't think I could take all that."

"But you're all bruised and bloody. We need to take you to the hospital. We don't have any choice. We have to get you some help. We have to report it."

Another storm moved across Rachel's face.

"Report it? Why? To make me more of a victim! Do you want everyone else to know about tonight? Are you that stupid? I refuse to continue to be a victim. No!"

I wasn't sure what to say, how to counter her reluctance to report the crime. I couldn't help but think she wasn't telling me the whole story, that I was missing some important detail. *But what?*

"I'm sorry, Rachel. I didn't . . ."

"It's okay," she said. "I didn't mean to yell at you. I just don't need anything else to deal with right now. Okay? I mean, gosh Alex, I just don't know. I went with him. I came here, alone, with him. I knew deep down what he was capable of, but I came anyway. So, in the end, it would be my fault. And, you and I would suffer for it."

I took her hands in mine and pulled her towards me.

"It's okay. We'll come up with something."

She knew I was lying, but at that moment, there didn't seem to be any other option.

I didn't see anybody riding to our rescue.


JUST SO YOU KNOW, God has a warped sense of humor. The night of Rachel's attack, as I walked around in circles for what felt like hours, trying to figure out a way to save our scalps, who knew God would be listening. Or that he'd decide to pitch in and help us.

But just for the record *(and to keep the Almighty on my side)*, my prayers were answered, though God couldn't resist slapping me upside the head in the process.

You see help arrived in the form of the biggest bunch of weirdos southeastern Oklahoma has ever seen. I'd just finished wiping what I hoped was the last of the blood off my face, when the front door of the old cabin creaked open. I whirled around, a little worried that maybe I was going to get that chance to take Danny's temperature for Rachel after all.

"Pssssst. Anybody here?"

I knew that voice. Through the mist, a huge, orange tennis shoe emerged. Whoever it was it definitely wasn't Danny.

"Hello?" The voice whispered. "Somebody in there?"

The door opened wider.

"Guys," the voice said, "I think I found where the noise was coming from. There's a light on in here."

I stepped from the shadows.

"Oh man! Gus! It's you!" *Did I look as relieved as my voice sounded?*

"Alex? What are you doing here?"

"Oh I don't know. Went for a stroll. Needed to try and find myself . . . this seemed like the perfect place."

Gus rolled his eyes. "You're here trying to do *what*?"

"For gosh sakes Gus, I'm kidding. Come on in. I need your help. All the help I can get!"

"What happened?" Gus looked at me, took a step forward, and then wrinkled his nose. "How come you don't have a shirt on? Man! This place smells awful. What a mess!"

Gus spewed questions, like a lit Roman Candle sputtering across a Fourth of July night: "How long have you been here? Why's the door busted? Where's . . ."

"Will you please shut up for a minute?" I said. "I told you I don't have time to explain. Rachel's been hurt!"

Instant silence. Gus stomped the rest of the way into the room. He waved a chubby arm and threw an order over his shoulder.

"Trev! JimBob! Get in here quick. It's Alex. And Rachel.

"They're in trouble!"

# CHAPTER TWENTY-TWO

YES, IT WAS TEAM DOOFUS: Gus, Trevor, and JimBob. Go figure. I'd never been so happy to see anyone in my life. I watched, amazed, as the three of them filed into the room, each looking more confused than the guy before him.

"What in the world happened?" Trevor finally asked.

"It's a long story . . ."

Before I could say any more, Gus spied Rachel. He raced to her, tossing stuff left and right to clear a path. When he reached her, he gently placed her hand in his big paw.

"Rachel, sweetie? What happened . . . are you okay?"

"Yes, Gus. It was . . . never mind, I'm okay now."

Gus's face morphed into a confused scowl.

"Alex, did you . . ."

I slapped myself in the forehead *(mostly to keep from slapping Gus)*. "Heck! No! Will you be serious? It was Danny!"

I watched as the light clicked on in his brain. Trevor gasped and made a move as if to help Gus shield Rachel. Behind them, a dark scowl spread over JimBob's face. I had never seen him so mad.

Gus didn't need to hear any more. His face was dead serious. "Okay. Okay. How can we help?"

IT TOOK ABOUT TEN minutes to explain what had happened, by then it was pretty obvious Rachel didn't like the replay.

"We gotta get her some help," Gus said. "Her pulse is racing. She looks pale, too."

Trevor looked around, sizing up the scene of the crime.

"This place is a mess."

"Don't touch anything," JimBob cautioned. "We need to take note of exactly what the place looks like and where everything was when we came in."

That made sense, because—despite Rachel's reluctance to have anyone know what Danny had done to her—I knew we couldn't get Rachel the medical help she needed without telling someone what had almost happened here tonight. I turned in a circle. *Where to start?* The snakes in my gut were on fire. I felt like I might puke or, worse, pass out in front of Rachel and the guys.

JimBob walked over to me. He seemed calm, in control. And he quickly confirmed my reading of the situation.

"Okay, Alex, relax." He pointed to me, then Rachel. "You take Miss Rachel to the hospital. Sorry Rachel, but we have to take you to the hospital. You have to be checked by a doctor. Danny could have seriously hurt you."

Rachel gave a reluctant nod.

JimBob turned his attention back to me. "Bud, you're going to have to hold it together. Tell 'em what happened and make sure you talk to the cops. There's no other way, trust me; she needs to see a doctor, and she needs to see one soon. Got it?"

"Got it," I said. "Sorry, I didn't know what to do at first. It's like everything is spinning out of control."

"Well, trust me. I know how to handle this."

"Yeah?" I looked at him for confirmation.

JimBob patted me on the shoulder.

"Ya know, Alex. That's what I like about you. Sometimes you're just like the rest of us—stu-pid. My uncle happens to be the camp's groundskeeper. He works here. That's why I come every year. He lives about five minutes away. He's going to help us."

*Yes, crime stoppers, this is how our hero, Alex, realizes there's more than freckles and gray soup between Hillbilly's ears. Tonight see the amazing Alex Anderson realize he's been a complete tool!*

"Do you think he would help us?"

JimBob smiled reassuringly again—a white picket fence of pearly teeth stretching from ear to ear. "Uncle Joe will help." Jim-Bob said it with all the confidence of a man who knows what he brings to the table. "And he's pretty tight with ol' Redding."

"So what do the rest of us do?" Gus asked.

JimBob took over. He sent Trevor out to look for Danny. Sent Gus back to the cabin to get a camera to record the scene. And then he ambled over to Rachel, his long face dark and serious.

"I'm real, real sorry you got hurt, Miss Rachel."

He reached out to give her shoulder a reassuring pat, but Rachel jerked away. Her arms covered her chest, like armor. But she didn't scare JimBob.

"Hey, it's okay. Don't you worry about nothing. Between the four of us." JimBob made a lasso in the air. "We'll take care of everything. Ain't nobody going to hurt you anymore, I promise. But you need a doctor, sweetie. And you're going to have to be brave. Okay? Can you do that?"

Rachel gave him a weak smile. "Yeah, I . . . I think so."

JimBob pulled a small silver cell phone out of his pocket. He flipped it open and punched in a few numbers, then after a few seconds he started talking to someone on the other end.

"Debbie? Hey, it's JimBob. Yeah. No, I'm okay. Look I need

your help ASAP. Somebody attacked one of the girls here. Yes ma'am. We're bringing her in now. She's fine, I think, but she's pale and frightened."

JimBob waved his arms and walked around in a tight circle as he recapped the highlights of the night's attack. "Yeah, it was an attempted rape. Her name is Rachel Clark. She's pretty bruised up. Okay. They're on their way."

I shook my head in wonder. "How in the world?"

"Like I said, I know people here."

JimBob flipped his phone open again, made another call, and waited for whoever was on the other end to answer. "Hey ol' man, did I wake you? Yeah, well, get yer tired self outta bed, 'cause we got problems. Meet me on the girls' side of camp at Cabin Number 3. Yep. I'm here now."

He hung up the phone, grabbed my arm, and pulled me to the back of the cabin. "Now listen here, cowboy. When you get to the hospital, a big gal named Debbie is going to meet you at the emergency room door. Deb is a retired SANE nurse."

"Huh? What's a SANE nurse?"

"She used to work at a battered woman's shelter. SANE stands for sexual assault nurse examiner. They can treat the patient and take the evidence that will help the police arrest the attacker. She knows exactly what to do. She'll help you."

"But they'll report it. Rachel isn't going to be happy about that. Will I get arrested? I mean I kicked Danny around pretty good."

"Yeah, it sounds like you came darn close to killing that ol' boy."

He was smiling, but I was red with fear and embarrassment.

"Yeah. I sort of exploded."

JimBob patted me on the back, as if he understood why and how my devils had come unleashed. "Hey, no sweat. If I'd been here, I'd have done the exact same thing."

"But what about the police?"

"Well, Alex I figure it like this." JimBob pointed to Rachel. "She's going to tell the cops you saved her. And she's going to tell 'em who tried to rape her. And we are here to back up her story, so you should be okay."

"Thanks, Hill . . . I mean, JimBob."

"No need for thanks. Now, listen. Uncle Joe will drive you guys to the hospital. Rachel's going to need you for support. You hang on to that little gal and make sure you don't leave her side. Got me?"

JimBob walked towards the door.

At the entrance, he turned back, pulled his T-shirt over his head, and tossed it to me. "You'll need that. Trust me."

I smiled, wryly. "Where are you going?"

He motioned towards the darkness.

"Me? I'm going to go get Redding out of bed. He and I need to discuss the lack of security at this place."


IF THEY GAVE OUT LETTERS for coming to the rescue, Trevor and Gus would have made the varsity squad. Both of them did everything they could to help us, and, when JimBob's uncle arrived, they carried Rachel to his car, then helped me slide her inside, so she felt as little pain as possible.

"Will you call us when you get there and tell us how she's doing, Alex?" Trevor asked. He gulped air for a second or two, then puffed on his inhaler. Tense situations made his breathing even worse.

"As soon as I know something."

Gus turned to Rachel. "Alex will take good care of you, okay? You don't need to worry about anything else."

For a moment I believed him.

Gus couldn't have been more wrong.

# CHAPTER TWENTY-THREE

FOR THE SECOND time in less than a year, I was going to the hospital emergency room, because someone I cared about was hurt. But at least this time I was able to hold Rachel and feel her next to me on the ride to the hospital. She clung to me, as if she was afraid that any minute Danny might reappear.

For his part, JimBob's Uncle Joe was great. He was gentle and kind and told Rachel over and over not to worry. I didn't think about it at the time, but by remaining calm and not acting frightened, he helped Rachel on what could have been one of the longest rides of her life.

As we drove, I thought about how much my life had changed and how, at the same time, it had stayed the same.

In the dark, I felt Rachel's fear as if it was my own.

I didn't even ask myself how that was possible.

Debbie, the nurse JimBob had told us about, met us at the door. She didn't look like a nurse. She looked like a fullback looking for a game. She was built square with a solid jaw and no neck. Her hair was brownish-blond. As we walked into the building, she gave a little nod to JimBob's uncle, after that she focused only on Rachel.

I hung back feeling stupid and helpless.

"Is there anything I can do? I'm her, ah, I'm her . . . "

Uncle Joe turned toward me. "Alex, I'm going to go back and see if I can be of any help at the cabin. Debbie will take care of you. She's good people. You and Rachel are in good hands."

Debbie helped Rachel into a wheelchair, and they started down the hall. I followed trying to talk to Debbie, but she wouldn't say a word to me. Instead, she leveled a glare at me that could have melted steel. For a second, I didn't understand. And then I did.

*She thought I was responsible.* It hit me like a brick to the face. She'd treated all sorts of rape victims. She'd probably seen this many times before: the guy brings the girlfriend to the hospital acting all nice and sweet, when he's actually the bad guy, the rapist, or the guy who beat her.

I felt cold. I wanted to scream "I'm not that guy," but I couldn't get the words out. It didn't matter. I couldn't get her attention anyway.

"I, we . . . I heard her in the cabin and went in . . . he was . . ."

Debbie shook her head.

"Not now," she said. "Tell it to the cops."

In my guts, the snakes squirmed.

"But I didn't . . ."

Rachel turned toward Debbie.

"Please, Alex is the one who saved me. If it hadn't been for him I might be dead. He fought Danny. He kept him from raping me." Rachel reached for my hand. "Please don't make him leave. I need him right now."

In that brief second, Debbie transformed. Her face softened. She found her voice. She even patted me on my shoulder.

"Good boy," she said. "I glad she said something, 'cause I was ready to put you away."

Next to me, Rachel squeezed my hand.

Despite my begging and Rachel's pleas, however, Debbie

wouldn't let me stay for the exam. She was adamant that it was against the rules.

"I have to give her a forensic exam," she said. "It's very delicate and very personal. It's not something you can be there for, I'm sorry, Alex. Besides, the law requires me to speak with Rachel privately. I hope you understand."

I was trying to understand. I gave a little nod of agreement.

"Okay, just please take care of her."

"She'll be fine. Seems to me she has a good man in her corner. And, I promise you I won't let a thing happen to her."

With that, Debbie eased Rachel into a wheelchair and pushed her through a set of swinging doors. I retreated to the waiting room, where I tried to clear my head. All of this was so familiar—the smells, the sounds, the noise, the bustling doctors and nurses. I hadn't been there very long when a tall, gray-haired doctor walked over to me.

"Are you Alex Anderson?"

"Yes sir."

"I'm Doctor Phillips," he said. "We need to make sure you're okay."

He led me to a smaller exam room at the end of the hall.

"It's okay. We just want to check you over."

I hopped up on the table, and the doc got started. He cleaned the blood off my face (*would I ever get it all off?*) and asked me where I hurt. I told myself I must not have been as bruised as I thought, if he had to ask me such a question.

"Will you take off your shirt please?"

I shook off JimBob's T-shirt. The doc put his stethoscope against my back and told me to breath.

"You have some extensive bruising, young man. Can you tell me what happened to you?"

"I was trying to keep a friend from being raped."

The doctor stopped. I felt his hand tighten on my shoulder.

"It looks like it," he said. "Where is the person who did this?"

"He ran off before we could stop him."

The doctor didn't say anything else. Instead he finished his exam and scribbled a prescription on a small notepad.

"I wrote out this prescription for a painkiller," he said. "It looks like you were punched in the kidneys. I could tell more with a CAT scan."

"Please, not right now. I mean I feel okay. I don't think it's that bad. Besides I'm worried about Rachel, the girl I brought here. Can you check on how she's doing? I promise if I start to feel bad I'll come back."

The doc stood silently for a second considering my proposal, then nodded in agreement.

"Okay, give me a second. I'll see what I can find out."


I STEPPED OUT OF THE exam room and into the hall, where I found an empty chair. The fear was overwhelming. It was Stillwater all over again. A few moments later, I saw the doctor walking towards me. I held my breath as he approached.

"You're friend is okay," he said. "She's with Debbie, one of our nurses."

He pointed to a large, ugly waiting room.

"They're waiting for you over there."

I walked down the hall toward a circle of light and the rumble of a late night television show. As I drew close to the waiting room, Rachel spied me. She jumped up and off the couch and ran to me.

"Are you okay?" she asked.

"Yeah, the doc just wanted to check me over," I said. "I'm fine. How about you? The doctor told me you'd be okay. Is that true?"

Rachel laid her head on my chest.

"The exam was horrible," she whispered. "It was worse than a trip to the gynecologist."

"Are you really okay?"

"I'm okay," Rachel said. "Debbie was sweet and talked to me

through each step of the procedure. She said she was able to collect a bunch of evidence, but it's not something I want to ever repeat."

I rubbed my face. I was tired and uncertain what to do next.

"So what do we do now?"

"I'm not sure," Rachel said. "Debbie said we're supposed to wait here. She said she'd be back in a minute."

She sat back down on the cheap plastic couch. I sat down beside her. Rachel leaned against me, then put her lips softly, against my ear.

"Alex. I just want you to know that without you, I would never have made it," she whispered.

"Shhhh, it's okay," I said. "You're safe now."

I pulled Rachel against me. We sat there quietly for a few seconds. Suddenly, her body went rigid, like a hunting dog that has spotted a rabbit. She jumped up from the couch and ran towards the opposite hall.

"Rachel, what the heck?" I looked up.

Running down the hall, accompanied by two policemen, were Mr. Redding and Rick. And they were heading straight for me.

# CHAPTER TWENTY-FOUR

THE FACES OF THE COPS, Mr. Redding, and Rick all looked the same, like they'd eaten a handful of broken glass. I stood and held up my hands. I wanted to say something, but a policeman with a square jaw and gray eyes stopped me.

"You need to sit down young man."

He grabbed my arm and shoved me back into the chair.

"But, if you would just listen . . ."

Rick looked at me like he'd never seen me before.

"Alex. This is serious," he said.

"But you don't understand. It wasn't . . . I was just . . . I was just hiding from the rain when I heard a noise." I pointed down the hall. "Rachel is here. She'll tell you."

Mr. Redding shook his head. "Alex, we have witnesses. Your clothes are bloody and torn."

"It wasn't me!"

The cop grabbed me by the throat, pulled me out of the chair, and shoved me against the wall.

"Why don't you just shut up?" he hissed.

Mr. Redding waved him off. "That will be all officer. We're in a hospital. That's not necessary."

The grip on my throat relaxed. My toes felt for the floor. I sat down, and Mr. Redding joined me.

"Alex, you must tell me the truth. One of my students has been assaulted. This is serious. You were there. Right now you are the main suspect. Several others saw you out after curfew."

"I couldn't sleep," I said. "I went for a walk, and I thought I'd go see Rachel. "

"Alex, stop!" said Rick. "You have to level with us; we need to know what happened."

"But you're not listening!" I shouted, trying to find someone who would. "I didn't do anything. I was trying to help Rachel."

Rick scowled; he looked more upset than when he'd walked in with the cops. "What? And you just happened to be there? Come on Alex, we're not stupid. We hear stories like this all the time."

"Ask Rachel, she'll tell you. She was just here."

"Where is she now?" asked Rick. "We were told she was being treated for an attempted rape."

I pointed to a set of white doors with the words "Emergency Personnel Only" marked on them in red.

"She's here. She went through there. Her nurse is Debbie. They said she is okay."

I buried my face in my hands. Despite how often it seemed to happen, it always amazed me how fast my life could spin out of control.

"Alex, you need to talk to us," said Mr. Redding. "Your entire future depends on the next few minutes. You must tell us the truth."

Slowly, I looked up. I couldn't tell if he was listening to what I was saying or if he'd already made up his mind. His face was so impassive. "I have told you the truth. You're not listening."

"Alex, even you would have to admit this story is highly unlikely."

"It wasn't me. I went for a walk and jumped up on the porch to get out of the rain. I heard a noise inside and…"

Mr. Redding pointed to the cops standing beside him.

"I'm afraid the officers are going to have to take you into custody until we can sort this out."

The bigger of the two officers moved towards me. He grabbed both my arms and jerked them behind my back. I tried to jerk away, but he twisted my arms until I thought he'd break them off. "The more you struggle the tighter I twist," he hissed.

I went limp. The cop stopped twisting. I felt cold metal bite into my wrists—handcuffs. I turned to Rick. I wanted to look him in the eye. I wanted him to know I knew he could have stopped it.

"I told you it wasn't me. After all you idiots figure it out, I'm out of here. I never want to see you or this place again."

The cop shoved me out the door and down the hall, eventually herding me outside. "Come on, punk," he said. "Time to go."

Through the glass door, Rick and Mr. Redding got smaller and smaller.


THEY TOOK ME OUT the back of the hospital, down three flights of stairs to a side parking lot. I couldn't believe it. I was being arrested. My mind raced. What were Bill and Clarise going to say? And what was going on with Rachel? One minute I'm holding her in the waiting room and the next she's running down the hall, like a startled rabbit. It was like she didn't remember I was there. For a moment, I thought it was some cruel game. I thought I'd been set up. "Nooo," I told myself. "Too much television. No conspiracy theories at work here."

*…tonight on the Alex Adventure Channel. See Alex Anderson get arrested, tried, and convicted for trying to stop a crime. Only in America!"*

The big cop yanked me to a stop by a black-and-white cruiser.

"Hold up, slick," he said. "This is your ride. Don't make it hard on yourself. Just get in, sit back, and shut up."

He pushed me towards the patrol car, opened the door, and started to shove me in the backseat. The screams stopped him.

"You have the wrong guy! Al, you have the wrong guy!"

The cop—yeah, his name was Al—stopped in mid push. He turned and looked towards the emergency room entrance. Across the parking lot, Debbie and Rachel ran toward us, waving their hands.

"What is going on?"

Debbie slid to a stop in front of the car. "Al, how could you be so stupid?" She pointed to me. "That boy didn't do anything."

Rachel raced to my window and pounded on the door.

"Oh, Alex, I'm so, so sorry. I didn't know. I was trying to . . ."

Al the cop stopped cussing long enough to scratch his head. He looked at me, then back at Debbie and Rachel.

"You're telling me this kid is innocent?"

Both women nodded their heads up and down like a pair of bobbleheads. (*Debbie in particular reminded me of one of those toy dogs you see in the rear window of a car.*) Rachel jumped in front of Al, waving her hands like she was at a southern Baptist prayer meeting. I expected any moment for her to shout "Amen."

"It wasn't him," she said. "He didn't do anything wrong. You have to let him go. He saved my life and you . . . you arrested the wrong guy. You can't lock him up like a criminal. He didn't do anything wrong!"

I could tell Al wasn't sure what to do. I was pretty sure he knew he was wrong, but Mr. Redding and Rick were nowhere around to confirm it. Rachel raced back to the cruiser.

From inside I watched her lean her forehead against the window in defeat.

# CHAPTER TWENTY-FIVE

FOR THE FIRST TIME in days, I felt normal. It had taken longer than it should have but the cops had finally let me go. Now with a hot shower, a big breakfast, and enough coffee to keep me awake for days behind me, I felt almost like myself. But the best part, the absolute best part, was that my room was air-conditioned. For the past two months, I'd lived in a cabin in which the air conditioner worked only when it felt like it. Most days, that meant the place was cooled by an ancient ceiling fan, and so most days by about two in the afternoon, the place smelled like a locker room. Not today. Today, my room was cold and dark and, for the first time in forty-eight hours, no one was screaming.

"WELL ALEX, IT WOULD SEEM we might have . . . I mean I might have . . . well, it would seem that we didn't have all the information."

Rick squirmed in his chair.

It was obvious he knew he'd screwed up. Badly.

"I kept trying to tell you, but you wouldn't listen."

I was still mad at them. The memory of my almost arrest was raw. And now, only a few days later, after Rick had done his "investigation," here we were. I was supposed to say no harm no foul and forget it, so we could all go back to being one big happy family. Yeah, right. Rick gave me a fake smile.

"I understand how you feel," he said. "I'd feel that way, too, if I were in your place."

Across the room, Mr. Redding remained silent. Occasionally, he looked at me, but he never said a word. He just returned to scribbling in his notepad. I pushed myself out of the chair.

"You understand? Really Rick? When was the last time a cop shoved you down the hall? When was the last time you were handcuffed and thrown in a patrol car? When was the last time you were accused of raping someone?

Rick looked at the floor. I wanted to throw something, but I knew it wouldn't help. Getting Rick's or Mr. Redding's attention would take something else. And I had no idea what that something else could be. I started for the door.

"Well, I can tell this conversation is over," I said.

Before anyone could respond, the door opened. Rick looked up. Mr. Redding dropped his pen.

"No, no, no, you shouldn't be here." Mr. Redding walked towards the door. "Rachel, we haven't finished here, and I don't think you should . . ."

Rachel pushed her way into the room. She stood with her hands on her hips. For a second I wasn't sure it was her, she looked so different. She stood like an amazon warrior goddess, ready to kick in a few heads.

"I need to talk to you." She pointed to Mr. Redding.

Mr. Redding sat back down in his chair and heaved a heavy sigh.

"Rachel, honestly, I didn't feel this involved you. We've been trying to contact your parents. I'll let you know when we reach them.

"I told you they were in Europe, somewhere in Scotland."

"I understand that," said Mr. Redding, "but until I speak with them, it would not be prudent for all of us to speak together about this. This conversation concerns actions between myself, Rick, and Alex. I'm not sure you should even be here."

"Come on Bill! For years you've been in my life—you're my dad's closest friend. You've been to my house a million times. And now, suddenly, you won't listen to me? That's just wrong, and you know it. This didn't happen to a stranger. It happened to Alex and me. And, you won't even listen to what I have to say.

"It's like this: My ex-boyfriend Danny Washington tried to rape me. He had me on the floor, and he tried to rip my clothes off. He punched and slapped and groped me, and he said he would kill me if I didn't do what he wanted. He tried to rape me!"

Her efforts to hold off the tears failed. Rachel's sobs filled the room, but she pushed through them.

"For whatever reason—fate, a guardian angel, or God, himself, Alex came in at the right moment. He saw what was going on, and he stopped it. He fought Danny until he was bloody and hurt, and he kept Danny from hurting me—from raping me. Alex saved me! Don't you see? He saved me. And you…"

She pointed to Rick, then back to Mr. Redding.

"And you had him arrested. Why?"

Mr. Redding looked at Rachel and then turned towards me.

"Rachel, I don't know what to say. We were wrong, and sometimes that can be difficult for an adult to admit. When I heard you were hurt, Rick and I raced to the hospital. I overreacted, probably because I do know you so well.

"Your father had charged me with taking care of you. And when we saw Alex standing there, all bloody, at the hospital, and maybe because we had few hard facts at the time, we made an assumption."

Rachel leaned against the door; her face hard and damp with tears.

"You assumed wrong, and you wouldn't listen to anyone else

tell you otherwise. Even after Alex begged you. Didn't JimBob talk to you before you went to the hospital? Why didn't you listen to him?"

"We had already left by the time JimBob returned to campus," Rick said. "And you're right. I didn't listen to Alex. I was so angry that nothing could have made me listen to him that night. I don't know what else to say, but, well, I screwed up. It's that simple. And I'm sorry I hurt you, Rachel, and you, too, Alex."

Rachel pulled me out of my chair. She put her arms around me.

"Alex saved me," she said. "He saved my life and he kept me from being raped. No one has ever fought for me like that. Even with all his pain, he fought for me—not once but twice. He took punch after punch for me.

"And day in and day out, he has listened to me, laughed with me, cried with me. He told me I was beautiful. He has cared about me. And he risked everything for me.

"I guess that's why I'm so angry. No one has ever loved me like that before. And it's like you are trying to take that away."

Mr. Redding folded and unfolded his hands.

"You're right, Rachel. You are absolutely right," he said. "We made a huge mistake, and both of us are truly sorry. I don't know what else to say."

"He's a hero," she said. "I just think he should have been treated better. I expected more from both of you."


OVER THE NEXT FEW WEEKS, I stayed close to Rachel. Despite their best efforts, neither Mr. Redding nor Rick could track down her parents. They did speak to Bill and Clarise, though. I was worried about what would come from that conversation, but Mr. Redding did what he said he would do and explained everything. Bill said I could come home if I wanted to. And, get this, I told him no.

After the come-to-Jesus meeting, we had a big, campus-wide confab, and both Mr. Redding and Rick apologized to me in front of the entire camp. "Alex Anderson is a noble, young man," Mr. Redding told everyone. "Despite intense pain of his own, he was willing to fight for someone he cared for—that's something we could all do well to emulate."

Mr. Redding also thanked Gus, Trevor, and JimBob. He said they were shining examples of true friendship and represented everything that is good about the world. I might not have gone that far, but I did agree with him that those three guys were the best friends a guy could hope to have.

After the assembly, Rachel and I strolled back to the cafeteria. Mr. Redding—at Rachel's request—was hosting a huge ice cream feed for the camp, and I didn't want to be late. Ice cream melts quickly when the temperature is ten degrees hotter than the sun.

"Come on Rachel! Let's go."

"Alex, slow down. What's the rush?"

I pointed at the cafeteria.

"Ice cream, silly. Redding bought chocolate and strawberry. And I'm not missing out on that."


FOUR DOUBLE DIPS LATER, I was stuffed but feeling good. The ice cream was great. Rachel was happy, and they'd canceled my reservation at the county detention center.

Life was better than it had been in a long time.

I'd just tossed my plastic spoon and cup in the trash, when I felt a tap on my shoulder.

"Hey pard, you save any for the rest of us?"

I smiled. I knew that voice.

"That sounds like William James Robert, I do believe."

"Ahhh, can't we go back to Hillbilly? It requires fewer words and has a better ring to it."

"What's up?"

JimBob leaned in, scanning the cafeteria crowd as if he was looking for someone.

"Hey," he whispered. "Where's Rachel?"

I pointed to a small circle of girls near the side door.

"She's over there with the entire population of Girls Cabin 2," I said. "I believe they're discussing the finer points of Red Ruby Number Five fingernail polish."

"You're insane Alex." But as he pulled me away from the crowd, his face turned dark and serious. "Well, that's good. I'm glad she's busy, because I wanted to talk to ya for a sec."

"Okay, shoot. What's wrong?"

"I just talked to Uncle Joe," he said. "He was talking to one of his cop friends—I think it was the smart one, not that idiot who tried to arrest you."

I pushed the image of my almost arrest from my mind.

"I didn't know there was a smart one."

JimBob laughed.

"Well, yeah, now that you mention it. Anyway, that cop told Joe they caught that douche-bag Danny."

I felt my eyes bulge in my head. "Really? When?"

"Early this morning, just across the Texas line. He'd been hiding out around the southern most tip of Lake Broken Bow, where the Mountain Fork River begins. He was heading for Dallas."

For the first time in a long time, I felt relief.

"That's great. Now, maybe, we can move on."

JimBob scratched his head; something in his manner made me give him a closer look. In my gut, the snakes rattled.

"Well, yeah, Alex, you can, see," he paused to spit a wad of tobacco juice into the trash can. "See, there's more . . . Danny's dead."

"Dead? What happened?"

"Not sure," JimBob said. "Cops ain't saying much. But Joe caught the story on his police radio that said the Broken Bow cops were trying to take a male suspect into custody this morning when the suspect bolted."

"They shot him as he was running away?"

"Actually I believe he shot at them first. But, anyway, they nailed him, and, well, he's dead. So Rachel won't have to worry ever again."

"Yeah, guess that solves that problem."

JimBob patted me on the back, like he understood how I could be torn between celebrating the return of Rachel's safety and wondering how a guy I'd seen just the other day could be dead.

"Just thought you ought to know."

I watched him walk away. And, for some weird reason, I felt sad. Don't get me wrong, I still hated Danny, and I sure hated what he tried to do to Rachel. But now, now that I'd had time to think about it, I was sorry I had beaten him so badly that night.

Images of the attack flashed by as if I was back in that cabin. I saw myself raising a piece of wood ready to kill another person. It was as if someone else was doing the punching. Someone I didn't know. I thought of all the fights I'd been in over the past few years, and, I had to admit, maybe Rachel was right. Maybe I was becoming a little too much like Danny. Maybe I was at the point where I just liked to slap people around.

Maybe I'd been mad for a long, long time.


THAT NIGHT, FOR THE first time in years, I talked to God. The snakes in my gut slept, so it was just me and him. I told him everything. I told him about my fear and anger, about how I missed Kev, and how I didn't understand why jerks get to live and good people die too young.

I told God I was worried about how much I had enjoyed kicking the living daylights out of Danny that night, how I now knew that I'd wanted to kill him. And I told him how weird I felt now that Danny was dead. I also told him about Rachel and how I felt about her.

I told him how I was drawn to her.

I guess, if I was a church-going person, I might have called it a prayer. But I'm not. Whatever it was I was pretty sure he listened, because after I was through, I slept, deep and hard, and the next day I didn't feel so strung out. I don't know much about religion. But that night, I knew for a fact that whatever you called him—God, Buddah, Yahweh—he was in my corner.

Maybe he had been there for a while now, because things seemed different . . . better. Now when I thought about all the fighting I'd done, it made me wanna blow my lunch.

So I made myself—and him—a promise.

I promised I would never again hit anyone in anger.

Now that didn't mean I wouldn't try to protect Rachel or somebody else I saw being attacked. But I was going to quit getting so mad that I wanted to kill another person.

That was what I told God. 'Cause we both knew I'd seen enough people die to last me a lifetime.

# CHAPTER TWENTY-SIX

FIVE WEEKS UNTIL camp was over. Thirty-five days, then it was back to Stillwater. If pressed, I'd probably admit that my time at Wha-Sha-She hadn't turned out so bad. I mean, some of it had been okay, if you didn't count the mud, the two fights, an attempted rape, and my short-lived career as a criminal.

Then there was Rachel. It took her time, but she came back to herself. She was tougher than she knew. And I like to think it helped that she knew she was surrounded by people who cared about her.

Rachel had even spent a weekend with Debbie, the SANE nurse. Debbie showed up at dinner one Friday, and the next I knew the two of them were off for the weekend. They stayed gone until Sunday, and when they returned, Rachel seemed happier.

I'm not saying the attack didn't change her. It did. She was jumpy. Easily startled. And, somehow, not as innocent and open anymore. Also, for some reason, she was now always in a hurry, like life had to be done quickly or not at all.

But what I could never understand was why she was more sensitive than ever about her past relationship with Danny. Since the night I told her Danny was dead, she had vowed never to mention his name again. She seemed so adamant about it, I figured she would stick to her word.

I was wrong.

"HEY HANDSOME! This seat taken?" Rachel asked, as she slid in next to me and pecked me on the cheek. The cafeteria was about half full. At the tables near us, campers looked at the food on their plates as if it were a bad science test.

"Well, I was saving this seat for this girl I like, but she's been ignoring me lately, so I'll probably just tell to her to get lost. If I ever see her again, that is."

Rachel slugged me in the shoulder.

"Alex, you are not very nice."

"Tell me something I don't know."

I pointed to her tray.

"That gray stuff—you probably wanna leave it alone. They still haven't arrested the guy who made it, so we may never know what's in it."

Rachel giggled.

"Oh, it's not that bad. See?"

She put a spoon full in her mouth. Honestly, I couldn't help it. Sometimes you just had to laugh. Just about the time she tried to swallow, her face took on a new expression, like someone had grabbed both her ears and twisted them in different directions. She frowned, gagged, and coughed. I laughed until I thought I'd explode. *Hey, I'd tried to stop her.* I pushed my tray over to her.

"Want some more?"

Rachel shook her head violently.

"No! Oh no!"

I could see she was trying not to hurl on my shoes.

"I've…had…plenty."

I slid a small dish of peaches in front of her. "If I were you, I'd skip the main course and go directly to dessert."

The peaches disappeared. And the ruckus in her stomach seemed to subside as well.

"So what's going on? I thought you had pottery with Brandy and Claire?"

Rachel gave me this look and then a wicked grin. "I skipped it."

"Cool. Wanna go for a walk or something?"

"I thought you'd never ask."

We bailed out of the cafeteria and headed for the lake.

"Did you wear your suit? We could swim."

Rachel stopped. Some emotion I didn't recognize flashed across her face. She looked weird, so weird. My mind immediately went to the dark side. Oh God! Was she freaking out still about the attack? I grabbed her hand. And about fifty million thoughts crashed my brain at once. Since the attack, navigating her emotional terrain had been like tiptoeing through land mines.

"Rachel, I'm sorry. Is something wrong?"

Rachel stared at me like the last of my brains had just rolled out of my head and onto the floor.

"What? No, silly. Nothing like that. I thought we could talk."

"Ahhh okay."

They were two words a guy usually doesn't like to hear, but with the summer we'd had, I could understand her need to talk better than maybe I once would have. Rachel plopped down on a rock, picked up a stick, and started drawing circles in the sand with it. I sat down beside her.

"Everything okay with you?" I asked, just to make sure I was reading her mood right.

Rachel smiled. "Well, yeah, I guess . . . but I'm not sure."

"I don't understand."

She was blushing now, and she looked embarrassed.

"Alex, there's something I need to tell you, but I'm afraid."

"Why? How bad could it be?"

Rachel drew a circle inside the one she'd just drawn.

"It's not, bad. It's just, well, if I don't tell you, I'll go nuts."

"So spill it."

She stood and reached for my hands. This was beginning to remind me of when my mom tried to tell me my dog, Rusty, had been hit by a car.

"Alex . . . I."

In one, swift move she was in my arms. She covered me like Christmas ribbon. Her face buried in my shoulder. I traced small circles on her back.

"I don't know how else to say this," she said, her voice muffled against my shirt, "so I'm just going to say it."

I felt a frown drift across my face.

"You're scaring me Rachel."

She reared back and put her hand over my mouth.

"Will you be quiet? Just for a second? I've got to say this now, or I never will. Okay?"

"Okay, shoot. I'm all ears."

"Alex, I'm . . . I'm in love with you. I've never told anyone that before. But I am. I'll understand if you don't feel the same way, but I had to tell you. Don't be mad at me."

Then Rachel reached up and pulled my face towards hers, super slow motion. Our lips touched. It was one of those kisses when everything slows down and you can see yourself standing there, but you are outside yourself, too. Definitely not your standard sixteen-year-old, trying-to-suck-your-lungs-out kiss. This was more of a gift, a kiss for a rainy afternoon interlude—no spit and hormones but soft, like a breeze.

It was a kiss to be remembered.

She tasted like peaches and salt. The little man who lives in my head bounced off the wall with joy. She'd kissed me! Even with my eyes closed, I could see her. I could see her pain, and her fear. I could see inside her. I knew exactly what she was thinking.

She loved me.

Talk about a miracle. She loved me. Me. The psycho-warrior

**155**

of Stillwater High. The poster child for screwed-up, slightly sui-cidal-but-always-ready-with-a-good-left-hook sixteen-year-olds. The guy who'd watched his best friend die. My head swirled. (*So this was what it felt like to be loved.*)

Her sweet voice brought me back to earth.

"Alex?" Rachel said. "I should tell you that while I've been afraid of saying anything to you, I've known this for some time."

I stood there. Silent. Clueless. Unfortunately, once again the little guy operating my brain had chosen an inopportune time to take a friggin' coffee break. What to say . . . what to say. I had no idea what to say. I didn't know the words.

Rachel was beginning to notice I hadn't said anything.

"Alex? Alex, are you in there? Are you mad?"

A slow, stupid smile drifted across my face, and I could feel the gears engaging in my head.

"No, gosh, no! I was just . . ."

Rachel pulled me towards her, and this time she didn't let go. She seemed calm, but I knew deep inside she was scared. It was like I could read her emotions, like she was inside my brain and inside my belly. It reminded me of Kev and me. How I used to be able to finish off his sentences for him. But this was a girl. I'd never experienced anything like this with the opposite sex.

Wow! For so long I'd dreamed about her. But now, now everything was different. Don't get me wrong, I still loved the way she wore a T-shirt. But it was more than that now. I wanted to hold her. I wanted to keep her safe.

"You're being awful quiet," Rachel said.

"Sorry. I'm just enjoying being here."

She nestled deeper into my chest. I felt her breasts rise and fall. She was relaxed. She seemed, well, almost peaceful. Inside me, a feeling moved from my belly to my head. I was swimming. Swimming to the surface of a very deep pool. I wasn't tense anymore. The snakes were gone. I stepped back and took both Rachel's hands. I could hardly believe it. She had actually said she loved me.

I wanted to say something back, I really did—something equally amazing. I wanted to let her know how I felt. But the words wouldn't come. Then, like they had a mind of their own, my arms moved. One tightened its hold on Rachel. The other pressed her hands over my heart, as the tears streamed down my face.

# CHAPTER TWENTY-SEVEN

FOR ABOUT A WEEK now I'd bounced around camp like a balloon. Rachel had said she loved me. That thought played on a continuous loop in my brain. It usually took something pretty serious to shake up ol' Alex but this? This I had not expected.

This afternoon, Rachel should have just finished crafts, so I wandered over to the cafeteria looking for her, but she was nowhere to be found. I finally spotted her by the tennis courts. When she saw me, she ran to me, like those girls with flowing hair on the shampoo commercials.

I was pretty sure I loved her. I mean, I'd never been in love before, so I couldn't be sure. But from what I'd read in books, this seemed like the real deal. I felt all protective about her and excited at the same time. Every time I saw her I wanted to hold her and touch her.

Before with other girls, I was more interested in sports and hanging out with Kev. With Rachel, most of me wanted to be with her all the time—to protect her, to have the chance to learn everything about her.

I had a funny feeling I was a goner.

"Going my way?" Rachel asked, with a grin.

I took her hand, and we headed for our spot on the old boat dock. It was late in the afternoon by now, and we had only a couple of hours before vespers. I didn't resent having to go to chapel anymore; I'd gotten used to the singing and the prayers. I now found the whole thing to be cool and peaceful. And sometimes afterward, I felt better, too.

"Hey, where are you going? The dock's that way."

Rachel was walking ahead of me now. She looked back when she heard my protest and gave me a sly, almost wicked smile. Now I was worried.

"I just want something a little more private," she said.

My head whirled at the possibilities.

"You amaze me," I said. "First the 'I love you,' now this. Are you sure you're not smokin' something? I mean you seem a little weird— great, but a little weird."

A dirt clod whacked me in the chest. Rachel picked up another one and gave it a little toss into the air; I couldn't tell if that one had my name on it or not.

"Alex, stop being that way. Just relax. I'm not going to hurt you."

The thought of this little bit of a girl hurting me made me smile. I was still smiling when we came upon a small storage shed by the lake. Like everything else here, it was old, and I was betting that the last time it was painted movies didn't have sound.

Rachel tugged on my hand. "Come on. This way."

We slipped inside the building, only to find a rusty canoe, a pile of cardboard boxes, and a mountain of life preservers way past their prime. On one side, on the wall, the late afternoon sun struggled to shine through a dirty glass window. Rachel led me behind the canoe and onto a large, blue beach towel spread out on the floor.

"Sit here," Rachel said. "That way, people can't see us if they open the door."

"Wow, you've thought of everything," I said.

She lowered her eyes, as if I had embarrassed her.

"I just wanted to be alone with you for a little while. Okay?"

I felt bad for making her have second thoughts about our little rendezvous. But Rachel didn't stay upset. We sat and talked for a few minutes, then kissed for a while. It wasn't making out, but something more relaxed and tender. Not that I was complaining, but I couldn't help but feel like there was something more Rachel wanted from me that she wasn't saying.

I shook off the thought. Only a fool would worry about something else, when he could be kissing Rachel.

I was no fool.

## CHAPTER TWENTY-EIGHT

WE TALKED FOR A LONG while, with Rachel extracting a blood oath from me that, no matter what, we would always be truthful with each other. Even if it meant we had to hurt the other person in the process.

"Okay, okay," I said. "Cross my heart and hope to die. Will that satisfy you?"

Rachel nodded happily. "I just want you to know that you can always trust me, and I want you to know that you can always believe me when I say 'I love you.'"

I hadn't thought of it that way. I realized now she was serious.

I put my hand over my own heart this time.

"I don't make too many promises," I said, "but I swear."

She seemed okay with that, but I still wasn't sure. There was something hanging over us, something she wouldn't say, but needed to express. I didn't get it, but right then I wasn't going to push the subject. Under the late afternoon sun, we sat in that small, dirty shed, and time stood still. Rachel scooted towards me.

"Do you remember last week, the day I told you how I felt?"

"Duhhh. Yeah, why?"

"Well . . ." There was a long pause, as she laced and unlaced her fingers over and over again. "Well, there's something else."

"What?"

"I never told you the rest of the story about my surgery. Did you wonder about it?"

"No. It just proved you were like everyone else here—except maybe JimBob—messed up in some way. And actually he is, too, if you count him wanting to be a lawyer. So yeah, come to think of it, I guess I figured everyone here was pretty crazy—you included."

Rachel smiled, then raised up on her knees, facing me. "Well, not exactly. I'm sorry I didn't tell you everything."

Now I was curious. Sorry? What the heck did Rachel have to be sorry about? I tried to put her mind at ease.

"Hey, you had an operation. You got a scar in return. There's nothing to be sorry about."

"I didn't tell you the whole truth."

"Come on, Rach, let's get back to the kissing—stop joking around."

Rachel reared back. "No, no Alex, I'm serious."

"Okay. It's okay. You're beautiful. You're perfect."

I pulled her to me for a kiss. The kiss was short—I wanted longer, but she stopped me.

"Seriously, Alex. Stop for a minute. I need to say this."

Her face was suddenly all serious and concerned. Frightened, actually. That got my attention.

"Okay, I'm all yours. What is it that you need to tell me?"

Rachel took a deep breath. "When I was a baby, I was born with only three chambers in my heart, not four like everyone else. At first, my parents thought they were going to lose me, but they found this amazing doctor and after three heart operations, I was okay."

Now she had my attention.

"Do you remember any of it?"

Rachel shook her head.

"No. I was just a baby, but my mom told me how my whole family traveled to France, so I could have the surgery by this Doctor Fontan. He'd developed the procedure and I was one of his patients. We even lived in France for a while, until I was about four."

"But that's great, right? You're okay now?"

Rachel nodded yes, but her hands trembled.

"Well I was. Then a couple of years ago I caught some bug—some super flu thing—and it messed with my heart. I got a bunch of new doctors. And, anyway, I got so sick I almost died."

I wasn't sure what to say, so I just sat there. Quiet.

Rachel rubbed her hands together.

"Things got to the point that the doctor told my parents not to expect a sixteenth birthday for me."

Suddenly, I felt stunned, like someone had just nailed me with a brick upside the head. It was hard to imagine this active girl sitting in front of me almost dying because of a faulty heart.

"But, obviously, you got better."

"Sort of," Rachel said. "I stabilized, but my doctor said there was so much damage that I needed a heart transplant. My heart was so weak they were afraid I would never leave the hospital."

I felt my eyes grow wider. I had not seen this coming.

"You had a . . . a heart transplant. That was the surgery?"

"Yes, about a year and a half ago," Rachel said. "I'm sorry I didn't tell you the whole story at first. I should have. I was on the donor list for a while. It's hard to find organs for people my age. When they finally found a donor heart, they did the transplant. That operation saved my life."

I rocked back on my heels and watched the dust dance in the sunlight. And I had a terrible thought. "Rachel, when Danny attacked you, could it have killed you?"

"Well, it didn't help. But no, I don't think so." She thought for a moment. "Well, it is important for me to have cuts treated as soon as possible—my immune system is weaker because of the transplant so I'm prone to infections. So I'm glad you guys didn't listen to me

**163**

when I said I didn't want to tell anyone . . . I wasn't thinking clearly at the time."

I felt like we had dodged a bullet.

Suddenly that new super protective urge I'd been feeling for Rachel came over me. I pulled her close. And I think I understood a little better why Mr. Redding had been so concerned about her—he wasn't being overly protective, he knew how vulnerable she was.

"So are you okay now?" I asked. "Does everything work? Do you feel okay? Is there a list of dos and do nots? Maybe, an owner's manual I could read?"

Rachel giggled. "Alex, honey, I'm fine. As for my heart, it's fine, too. No signs of rejection, and I feel good and have more energy than before the transplant. Of course, I take a medicine chest full of drugs every day. That's why my doctor thought a summer outside would do me good. Fresh air. Sunshine. Exercise."

Rachel explained that since her dad and Mr. Redding are friends, Mr. Redding offered to let her come to Wha-Sha-She for the summer, but her parents had worried that activities, like swimming in the lake might not be safe. Luckily, her doctor had said Lake Broken Bow was big enough and clean enough not to do her any harm, and he made Mr. Redding promise to carefully monitor what she ate. Ultimately, her mom and dad relented.

"So, that's why I'm here."

"I don't get it. Why were you so frightened? I could tell you were scared to tell me. Why?"

"Alex, I told you the first time. I'm like Frankenstein. I even have someone else's heart. I thought you should know, but I also thought it might freak you out. But you deserved to know, so there wouldn't be any surprises."

I smiled. I mean, after something like that, what do you say?

"I also wanted to share something with you."

And just as she said "something," Rachel sat back, reached down, and pulled her T-shirt over her head. She dropped it in a pile on the towel. Underneath, she was wearing a skimpy pink bra.

If she'd meant to shock me, she'd succeeded. She took my hand and, gently, placed it over her scar. "I know, it's ugly . . ."

She let the rest go unsaid. Was she kidding. There wasn't a male within say three or four planets who wouldn't have gladly traded places with me. Yet I wasn't focused on her amazing bod. It was her scar that begged to be touched. Gently, I traced it with one finger.

"I've been cut open so many times, and I have all these scars. It's horrible. My body is ugly, hideous. I'm so sorry."

Now it was time for me to smile. I shook my head.

"I knew it—you *are* crazy, just like the rest of us," I said. "Do you not know how beautiful you are? Your scar, well, it's just . . .you. It's your story. It makes you interesting. And, it's old news."

"You mean you don't mind it?"

"I don't even see it."

For a few moments, she just sat there in that hot, spider-filled storage shed, with a guy who was obviously about two loads shy of a full haul.

"*Really?*"

"Really," I whispered. "You know I think you're beautiful. I tell you that like what? Ten million times a day. And what's a scar? Who cares? We both have 'em, okay? It's just my scars can't be seen."

Our lips touched. There, with the sun streaming through the dirty window panes, we kissed again, only this time the kiss was silky and sweet and lasted much longer than the last one.

Rachel pushed up against me, and I felt the heat from her body. Small droplets of sweat dripped down her chest. I slid underneath her, and my hands traced the curves of her body. I touched her skin, her face, her belly, everywhere, trying to memorize the girl that I loved. And, somehow, along the way, that pretty pink bra came off.

Far off, in the distance, I swore I could heard Gus laugh.

I smiled to myself.

Yes, Gus, I'm a lucky man.

# CHAPTER TWENTY-NINE

TIME SEEMED TO STOP and the rest of the world faded away. Even now, I don't know what possessed Rachel to choose that time and place. I only know that for those precious hours, she was mine. I'd never felt closer to anyone in my entire life—not even Kev.

We walked back to camp in the twilight. Rachel stopped me under a tree and kissed me.

"Alex, for the first time in my life I feel like a real girl. You made me feel loved and you made me feel beautiful."

I leaned forward and kissed her neck.

"I'm tired of being afraid," Rachel said. "I want to feel happy and alive."

She told me I made her feel that way. She told me again that she loved me. And, yeah, I told her I loved her, too.

And after that, everything changed.

After that, we were pretty much *the* camp couple. Inseparable. Always talking. I learned all about her family, her mom and dad, and her two sisters. I learned more about what it was like to live with a donor heart and the virus that had made it necessary for her to get a transplant.

And I learned her last secret: because of the medicine and other complications, she could never have children, and how that had made her mom cry almost as much as the problems with Rachel's heart. Rachel also told me I was the only boy she had ever let see her scar (*the attack didn't count*) and the only boy with whom she'd ever shared all her secrets, then she told me that Mr. Redding had found her parents.

And then she told me they were coming to take her home.

TALK ABOUT WEIRD. For most of the past three months, all I could think about was getting the hell out of this place. One hazel-eyed girl later, and all I wanted to do was slow time down. Now, not only did I not want to leave Wha-Sha-She, but I also didn't want Rachel to go.

I wasn't ready for her to go home, and I damn sure didn't want to be at camp by myself. I could feel my old dark friend depression settling in. I should have known by now: Just about the time things start getting better, fate strikes.

I sat on my bunk, once more mad at the world. Maybe God was mad at me because I'd gotten all but naked with a girl before I was married. Well, if that was the case, then I was a little disappointed in him, too. And it was a shame. He and I had been doing pretty well. I'd been staying in touch regularly. And I thought we both enjoyed our talks. The sunlight streaming through my window was so bright it made my head hurt. I was getting ready to get up to close the blinds, when the room went dark. Hmm, that was strange. Must be clouds, I thought. Maybe an eclipse. Nope. Just my roommate.

"Hey Alex," Gus said, standing over me. "You don't look so good. You okay?"

"Yeah, I guess." I counted the circles in the cabin's worn rag rug. "Just kind of an off day."

Gus plopped down next to me.

"It will get better, dude. I promise."

"I hope so."

I wouldn't appreciate it until much later in college, after the roommate from hell, but Gus, JimBob, and Trevor were naturally easy to live with; they didn't care about wet towels on the floor or unmade beds. Gus was also the Zen-master at scamming food from the camp kitchen, so all summer we'd had chips and tons of salsa, while other cabins went without.

After we started hanging out and I learned more about all of them, I realized they were all warriors, and I'd seriously underestimated them all. Gus was now down to two hundred and seventy-five pounds, but he had once tipped the scale at four hundred. He planned to keep working the program until he hit his goal weight of two hundred. I eyeballed him and noticed he was now as much muscle as he was fat. Heck, he had bigger quads than me.

As for Trevor, well I came to appreciate that when he wasn't gasping for breath—bad asthma, the kind that kills—he was hilarious. He'd pop off, and we'd be laughing for hours. Of course once in a while, he'd get started and his asthma would kick in, and we'd all have to scurry to find his inhaler—he was always losing it. I never told him, but there were lots of times when Trevor reminded me of Kevin. Like last Tuesday, it was late (*it was supposed to be "lights out," but we had a good poker game going*), and everybody was talking and being stupid. I started telling this dumb joke and when I got to the punch line everyone roared, and Trevor goes, "Well . . . hell Alex!"

I couldn't get outside fast enough. I was standing on the porch crying my guts out, when I felt a hand on my shoulder.

It was Trevor.

"Hey, Alex, you okay?"

"Yeah, it's hard to explain."

"I didn't say something wrong, did I?" Trevor asked, looking like someone who had just lost their dog. " 'Cause, man, if I did, I'm sorry. I can be stupid at times."

"Naw. It wasn't you. I just remembered something, and I guess it got to me."

Trevor shuffled his feet, still concerned but hesitant to intrude.

"Well, okay, if you're sure," he said, "but you're sure there's not anything I can do for ya?"

"Naw, I'll be fine."

I wasn't mad at Trevor. Heck, Trevor was just being himself. It was just for a moment in there, he'd sounded exactly like Kev. Seriously, for a few seconds, I looked around expecting Kev to be standing there, giving me crap.

Anyway, I went back in that night, and we finished the game and had a few more laughs. I guess that means I'm doing better. It's not that I don't still miss Kev, but I don't lose it as often.

And that night I didn't want the guys to think I was some kind of crybaby. I had enough problems without that.

To their credit, none of the guys ever said a thing.

For that I will always be grateful.

# CHAPTER THIRTY

I T WAS MONDAY, and Rachel was supposed to leave Friday. Camp would end the week after that. Our final week together had begun. I had taken a bold stance on the subject: I didn't want her to go. Heck, I didn't want to go myself. But from the way everyone was acting, you'd think I didn't have a say in the matter.

Despite the funk her departure had put me in, we managed to make some memories. Rachel swore she didn't want to leave, but her parents had given her no say in the matter. She had doctor appointments and she had to get ready for school. It all sounded like lame excuses to me but whatever.

I tried to tell myself that with modern technology—cell phones, texting, e-mail—there was probably no better time in the history of the world for a long distance romance. Rachel lived in Amarillo and I was stuck in Stillwater. I could see the phone bills already.

Even Father Time seemed against me. All summer, time had crawled, but now that we were down to our last five days together, the hours and minutes flew by. I can honestly say it was messing with my head.

By Wednesday, Rachel and I had argued twice. Not serious fights, but fights nonetheless. I told myself it was just because neither of us wanted to leave. Rachel was crying a lot, too. From what I knew of girls, that wasn't out of the ordinary, but it bothered me.

Since Rachel had to leave Friday, we made plans to hit the storage shed by the lake Thursday night after lights out.

"I want to be next to you one more time, before I leave," she said. "I'm going to miss you so much."

Like every other day this week, Thursday went by quickly. Before I knew what was going on, it was seven and time for vespers. A couple of hours of free time afterwards, and it was lights out at eleven. Exactly thirty-two minutes later, I felt my phone buzz, with a text from Rachel: "I'm in. Hurry."

I slipped out of my bunk and slipped out the cabin door. The air was cool, and the clouds made the night a deep, velvety black. I hurried to the shed. A couple of days before, I'd helped JimBob move some stuff in there for the cook. While we were there, I'd moved a few of the extra boxes, covered the window, and made sure the door hinges were oiled. Once in a while I get things right.

I slipped inside the shed, eager to see Rachel.

"Rachel?"

From the back I heard, "Alex, here."

I wound around the boxes, and I headed to the far back wall. Rachel had her cell phone opened. In the dim light I could see her face. Her hair was pulled back, and she was wearing a simple white T-shirt and shorts. She took my breath away.

"Hi!" I said between kisses.

"Hi, I missed you."

"Me, too."

I watched her close the phone. The room became inky black. She pulled me in for a kiss—a long, slow, make-your-eyes-roll-back-in-your-head smooch.

All of a sudden all I could think about was the one time Bill tried to talk to me about sex. I remembered him stumbling over his words as he tried to explain to Kev and me the difference between "having sex" and "making love."

Now I thought I had an idea about what he'd been trying to say. There in that little building was someone I loved—a lot. And, yes, when I am with her, I thought about sex. But for the first time, there was something more—something that wasn't just physical, a kind of soulful connection.

Call me crazy, but it felt like a promise.

IT WAS ALMOST FIVE in the morning, when it became clear our time together was almost over. Rachel was curled next to me. We'd gone over all the plans for getting her home—how many times I was supposed to text her, when to call, stuff like that. She was also supposed to check on some academic bowl thingy for which she had applied.

We tried to keep it light, focusing on the future and not her leaving. But after a while, we both got tired of pretending not to be sad.

"So are you going to miss me?"

Too bad she couldn't see the look on my face; there would have been no need for an answer.

"Well that's a pretty lame question. You know I am. I miss you now, and you haven't even left."

"I'll miss you, too." She snuggled closer.

"Hey, Rachel?"

"Yeah?"

"Are you scared?"

"About what?"

"About going to the doctor?"

"Not really. It's not like being scared, just, sort of cautious. Besides, I've known Doctor Evans since sixth grade. He was the surgeon who did my heart transplant."

"How many doctors have you had?"

Rachel counted on her fingers. "Seven, counting Doctor Fontan."

"Jeez." I looked at her face.

"What?"

"Were you scared when you had your heart transplant?"

Rachel nodded, like she knew exactly what I was asking.

"I was terrified. I was sure I was going to die. The night before the operation, my folks and everyone were at the hospital, and it was okay. But after everyone left, that's when it got outta control."

"What did you do?"

"I . . . I prayed. And prayed. And prayed. I told God that I wanted to have a life, and a boyfriend, and get married, and have kids and all that stuff. I prayed that I wouldn't die. I prayed that I'd be able to see my friends and that everything would be okay."

"Did it help?"

"Yeah . . . yeah it did. I can't explain it, but after I finished I just laid there and looked at the stars through the window. I remember seeing the moon and the Milky Way, and then I had this intense feeling that everything would be okay. I just knew. It was God telling me he'd heard my prayer and not to be scared."

I touched her scar. "Can I tell you a secret?"

"Sure, silly."

"I didn't talk to God or anything like that until I met you. I mean, I went to Kev's funeral service at the synagogue—my parents made me, but I figured God had a lot more to do than worry about than me and my problems. I thought Kev's death had made that clear."

Rachel's fingers worked their way down my cheek. "Maybe he's been talking to you for a while, and you just didn't know it."

"Huh?"

She leaned close to my face and spoke slow and deliberately.

"Maybe God wants you to know that Kev is okay now and that you're going to be okay, too."

"Yeah, maybe, but like I said, for a long time we didn't talk much if at all. Now, well, now things are different."

I wanted to talk more, but I wasn't sure what the rules were about talking about God during a makeout session, so I changed the subject.

"So, how did they do the transplant stuff?"

"Huh?"

"When they did your transplant, what all did they do?"

"You mean the operation?"

"No, like how do you get a new heart? It's not like you can go to the meat department at Wal-Mart and pick one out. Can you?"

Rachel giggled.

"No you can't. I was on a waiting list for a donor heart. There's a national registry. Doctor Evans signed me up. Once you're listed, they try to find a donor heart that matches your specific genetic type—they like to give you a heart from someone near your age, so the heart will last your lifetime."

"Sounds complicated."

"It was—and is. Not many kids are signed up to be organ donors. I was on the list for a long time. It seemed like ages."

"So when did you find out you were getting a new heart?"

"It was October. My folks had gone to a Halloween party, and I was home. It was just me and my sisters. We were watching this scary movie when the call came. I remember I screamed when the phone rang, because I was so engrossed in the movie. When I answered it, it was Doctor Evans, and he was so excited. He said they'd found a heart."

For once I was glad Rachel couldn't see my face. I wasn't sure she would have liked the weird, what-the-hell look I knew I wore.

"That just seems so weird," I said.

"I know. It's almost morbid. Especially when you realize someone died, and now you're getting a part of that person's body."

"So do you know who . . . who you got your heart from?"

Rachel's voice went quiet. "No. They won't tell you unless they have permission from the donor's family. And getting permission is a big, drawn out process. All they would tell us was it was the heart of a boy about my age, about sixteen, I think."

"Wow. Some kid didn't make it. And you got his heart?"

"Yeah, believe me, I have thought about that a lot. I just hope whoever it was knows how grateful I am."

"You don't know anything else about him?"

"No. Just that it was a sixteen-year-old boy who lived in our donor region."

"Donor region?"

"Oklahoma, Texas, and Arkansas. They try to match donors to families in the area. There's less travel time involved, and it's a lot better on the organ and for the person who's having the transplant. An organ, say a heart, has to be transplanted in just a few hours. It's a pretty tight turnaround—even if everything goes just right. In my case, my folks missed their Halloween party."

"Amazing. I've never thought about any of that." I touched her scar. "I mean, I knew about transplants, but the details, well they are . . ."

"Amazing?"

"Yeah, amazing."

Rachel fell quiet. When she spoke again, I could feel the conviction in her words.

"For me, it was a miracle," she said, "because whoever it was saved my life. I promise you: I thank God for that person every night."

# PART THREE

# CHAPTER THIRTY-ONE

THE CAMP BUS SMELLED LIKE piss and sweat. We'd left Wah-Sha-She behind us a couple of hours ago. I would be home soon. Rachel was already gone, but there had still been a lot of good-byes to be said. Trevor's folks had come to get him; JimBob had decided to stay a little while longer and hang with his Uncle Joe. So it was just Gus and I on the bus ride home. Gus was crashed two rows back, snoring but sleeping like a baby.

I'd loaned him my pillow, and he'd returned the favor with a gift of two cold sodas. Not a bad trade, but the sodas didn't come close to lasting the whole ride. We would reach Oklahoma City soon, then it would be another hour to Stillwater.

I missed Rachel, but I felt like I knew her even better after meeting some of her family. I had tried out my "Hi, I'm the new boyfriend and you can trust me" look on her father, but I all got was "Beat it, I'm the parent" in return. To his credit, Rachel's dad—also a Bill—did greet me with his best formal handshake. Other than that, he pretty much blew me off. I could tell he wasn't thrilled his daughter had a boyfriend . . . new or not (*who could blame him given how well the last one turned out*). I also took away the impression that he didn't like me much. Rachel's sisters, Tara and Lauren, didn't help my cause any. They ran around camp like a pair of Tasmanian devils. Her mom didn't even come.

I could tell it bothered Rachel, because her smile began to fade. Her dad kept telling her it was time to leave and pulling her towards the car. Each time he did Rachel turned bright red and her looks grew more intense. I figured a fight was brewing, so I drifted away under this big tree, while Rachel cornered her father for a discussion. Actually, she ripped into him. Once in a while I heard her raised voice. Occasionally, she'd point my way. After a while, it got real quiet. Finally they both walked over to where I stood. Rachel glanced at me, winked, and looked her dad right in the eye.

"Alex, my father, William Clark, has something he'd like to say."

She sounded just like my mom when my dad has screwed up. Rachel's dad stared at his feet, then at me. It must have been a serious chewing out, because he looked as if he'd been told Christmas had been canceled. "Alex, I may have been a little hasty. Rachel told me how you protected her from that Danny fellow her first day here." He stuck out his hand. "I want to say 'thank you.'"

Okay, I know it may be weird, but at that moment I understood the man. I could tell how much he loved Rachel, and, with everything she'd been through, I was pretty sure he was still worried about her. I shook his hand firmly, the way Bill had taught me. "I was happy to help. I think your daughter's, well, she's everything to me."

Rachel's father smiled, and he didn't say a thing when Rachel pulled me close and kissed me right in front of him. Of course, her sisters squealed and laughed and made stupid cracks. But yes, I was, officially, *the boyfriend*.

And everyone knew it.


THE DRIVE HOME SEEMED TO take hours. Gus, Trevor, and I had made plans to get together in fall. Gus lives in Guthrie just down the highway from me, and Trevor said he'd make the trip in from Tulsa. They both thought an Oklahoma State football game might be just the incentive they needed, so I was pretty sure I'd be seeing them again come fall. We were friends now, and friends, well, friends stay in touch.

The trip home Friday was only supposed to take a couple of hours. It took way more. The driver got lost—not once but twice—and we had to stop for directions both times. That combined with no air-conditioning in the middle of August, and you can imagine the stink. The only break from that long sorry ride were Rachel's text messages. She sent fifty of them—most goofy—but it was cool. At some point either her thumbs gave out or we lost service, because for about an hour it was just me, my fellow passengers, and a long, winding road.

No big deal. I was beat anyway. I pushed my duffel bag to the corner where the chair met the wall and slid down in my seat. We'd finally hit the Interstate and with most of the windows open, it was just tolerable enough to nap. I'd dozed off when my phone vibrated; it was another message from Rachel. This text was short and to the point: "Call me whn U gt bk—impt! R." (Translation: call me when you get back—important! Rachel)

I punched in "OK," hit the send button, and laid back down. We'd just passed Norman. My parents had said they would pick me up in Oklahoma City. I sure hoped they'd be on time.

WE HIT THE PARKING lot of Bishop McGuinness High School at half past the hour. Seven minutes later I had all my stuff piled on the sidewalk ready to go. Bill and Clarise were nowhere to be found.

I wasn't too thrilled about waiting for them, but anything was better than getting back on that bus.

Since I'd kinda figured they would be late (*they are always late for everything*), I bummed a ride with Gus and his folks to a little convenience store down the street from the school. With my last couple of bucks, I paid for a soda and some chips.

When we got back to the school, Gus was worried about leaving me by myself. "Hey, Alex, we can wait with you. I mean, if you, want us to."

"Naw, I'm good. I knew my folks would be late. They always are. Besides, they'd call me if there was a problem."

We went back and forth like that for a few minutes. Finally, I promised Mr. Wheelock, Gus's dad, that I'd call them if my folks didn't show soon. After they left, I actually missed Gus. I'd gotten used to him being around and now he wasn't. At camp, when Gus and I talked, my stories often were about Kev and me. I didn't even realize I was doing it, but Gus, well, he understood. He'd laugh at all the right parts and told me how cool he thought Kev was. I didn't realize how much about my friendship with Kev I'd shared with Gus, until right before he left with his folks.

He'd grabbed me in a bear hug that I was sure would snap every bone in my body.

"Man, Alex, I liked hanging out with you at camp. You were the best. I mean it. I'm glad you're my friend, and I promise that I won't forget you."

That made me smile, because I knew he meant it.

After the Wheelocks left, I found a shady spot under a big oak, leaned back against my bag and tried to call Rachel. All I got was her message: "Hi, you've reached Rachel Clark. I know your message is important, so leave your name and number, and I promise, I really, really promise that I'll call back."

It had to be the dorkiest phone message I'd ever heard. Being the funny guy that I was, I responded in kind: "Good afternoon, this is Special Agent Phelps of the Federal Bureau of Investigation, Oklahoma City Branch. We're holding Mr. Alex Anderson on suspicion of treason. Please return our call immediately."

Kev would have loved it.

After about an hour, Bill and Clarise still hadn't arrived. And I started to wonder if they'd forgotten today was the day? Then I realized that was ridiculous. Bill doesn't brush his teeth without a schedule. I flipped open my phone, ready to try Gus, when I saw the silver Buick. There was Bill. And Clarise. And Jenny.

And for the first time in ages, I realized I'd missed them all.

# CHAPTER THIRTY-TWO

THE RIDE HOME wasn't too bad. Bill didn't say much, and what questions he did ask he kept short. More than once he made a point of telling me how good I looked. Clarice smiled and said she'd missed me and was glad I was home. Even Jenny seemed happy to see me.

"Ohhh," Jenny said. "You have a great tan."

I rolled my eyes. I was gone for three months and all she noticed was whether or not I looked like a well cooked Thanksgiving turkey. Maybe things weren't so different after all.

We walked through the door of our home at about eight. The living room was dark, quiet, and cool. I dropped my bag in the foyer and quietly thanked the old dude who invented air-conditioning. For three months I'd sweated morning, noon, and night, and tonight for the first time in ages I was cool and comfortable.

I grabbed a soda—also ice cold—and hit the couch. Clarise sat next to me. She smelled like sandalwood and, for once, seemed happy. She tugged on my arm and pulled me close to her. "I missed you," she said. "I missed you every day. I was so worried about you.

I worried that you'd hate that place and . . ."

Her voice trailed off, leaving her worries about me to hang in the air. I thought I knew what she was trying to say, but I kept my mouth shut. It was nice, just sitting there with her. Nobody was mad and everything was peaceful.

Of course, that couldn't last.

Clarise started in with a few, simple questions, like "How was the center?" and "What did you do every day?" and "Did you make any new friends?" Softball questions. I must have answered them too easily, however, because just as I was about to doze off, she nailed me: "So who is this Rachel?"

"Huh?"

"Rachel. Who is Rachel? Is this a girlfriend? Someone you met? Who is she?"

Her questions came at me, like machine-gun fire. I'd known I would have to tell them sometime about Rachel, but I wanted to do it my way, on my own schedule. What freaked me out was that my mom even knew Rachel existed. I pushed myself deeper in the couch and bought myself a little time with a last slug of my soda.

"How do you know about Rachel?"

Clarise gave me her I'm-your-mother-and-a-great-detective look, before admitting she'd been privy to a few clues.

"Well, that's easy, silly boy; she's called here about five times since Thursday."

"Is she your girlfriend? Because she was very polite and sweet, and if she is, I think, that's wonderful."

Now it was my turn to smile.

"You mean you're not mad, because I didn't tell you?"

"No, honey." She ruffled my hair. "You've been so hurt for so long. Anyone who can make you smile is tops in my book. So tell me about her."

As I started to answer, Bill came in.

"Yeah, I'd like to know about this mysterious Rachel, too."

He dropped down next to me on the sofa.

"Don't tell me you've talked to her, too?"

"I've talked to her twice. She sounds cute."

Okay, so I was cornered. Bill and Clarise had me in their line of sight, they weren't mad, and I'd just been informed they'd talked to my girlfriend. I felt like a laboratory rat. It wasn't like I was embarrassed or anything. And they had paid for the trip that led me to Rachel, so maybe I did owe them something.

So I talked. I told them almost everything—though I didn't tell them any more than they already knew about Danny trying to rape her. I talked a lot about how much fun she was, and even told them a couple of stories about Gus, Trevor, and JimBob.

And, get this, I actually made both Bill and Clarise laugh. About an hour-and-a-half later, I could tell they were fine with me having a girlfriend, and they didn't seem as angry with me as they had been when I left home at the beginning of summer, so all in all it was a good night. I thought we were in the clear. I was wrong.

> *This week, on "The Amazing Story of Alex," we see the screwed-up moron with the weird parents has survived high school and hooked up with a girl! Now on Channel 47! Don't miss it!*

I'd just walked back into the kitchen, put my soda can in the trash, and started upstairs to bed, when both the parental units stopped me at the staircase. Bill put a hand on my arm.

"Son, I can't tell you how pleased I am that you found someone to talk to at camp. I can tell it helped. You seem much better."

I stood there with this half smile on my face, while my mom chimed in. "We know things have been difficult for you, Alex. But we want you to know how happy we are you're back home now, and how much we love you."

Okay, cool. They were happy; I was happy. Maybe things wouldn't be so uncomfortable after all. I missed Rachel and, yeah, even Gus, Trevor, and JimBob, but it was pretty cool that my folks were in a good mood, and, for once, my house didn't feel like a prison. I was just about to say "thanks" and go hit the rack, when Bill nailed me for the first time of the evening.

"Oh, Alex."

"Yeah?"

His face turned stern; Bill was back in "I'm the father" mode. "Like I said, your mother and I are pleased you've met someone. And, she seems nice on the phone, but I must insist you . . ."

My brain—what was left of it after hours on the bus—spun into overdrive. I'd thought everything was fine. What was wrong now?

"Ahhh, I . . . I . . ."

Clarise put her hand over my mouth. "Alex, maintain. Take a deep breath. All we're asking is that you call Rachel back. She has called here several times today, and it sounded important. Relax. Repeat after me: 'You are not in trouble.'"

Bill laughed. Loudly. He was pretty proud of himself. He smiled and handed me the telephone.

"Yes, here's the phone, please go call your girlfriend."

He stretched out "girlfriend," like some kid at school making a point would have said it. I wasn't sure whether I should laugh or be ticked. I watched the two of them walk back into the living room, laughing like Rachel and I do when we've just shared a joke. Amazing. I didn't think they had it in them. One minute they're sending me away, because I'm so screwed up, and the next they're reminding me to call my new girlfriend. Go figure.

What a long, strange day it had been. But if my dad had taught me anything, it was not to keep a hot girl waiting. I punched in Rachel's numbers and headed upstairs to my bedroom.

Downstairs, the two-person party continued.


RACHEL ANSWERED ON the second ring. Man, I missed her.

"Hey, you, it's about time. Didn't your daddy tell you never keep a Texas girl waiting?"

She sounded happy. A good sign, I thought. I was worried about this long distance stuff; I mean we'd spent almost every day together for three months, and now, we were going cold turkey on seeing each other. What if she found somebody else? What if she changed her mind? I shoved the negative thoughts away and tried to concentrate on the sound of her voice.

"Sorry, I just got in a while ago. I was getting ready to call you, but my parents cornered me with a lot of questions. I swear."

"I know, silly. Don't worry. I guess I made a nuisance of myself. I called your house several times today, but in my defense, I missed you. And, it was nice to talk to your mom and dad."

"Yeah, Bill and Clarise said you'd called. What'd you talk about?"

"Alex, just relax, okay? We just talked. I told them how wonderful you were, and how kind and sweet you are. That's all."

"Wow, you make me sound good."

"Oh, stop. Now listen. I need to tell you something, okay?"

"Sure, you have my full attention. What's up?"

"Everything. Everything's up. It's perfect."

"Huh?"

"Alex, you remember that academic competition I mentioned?"

The last two weeks she was at camp, Rachel had been obsessed with this academic bowl, the Southwest Scholastic Competition. She'd applied in the spring, and she was starting to freak out, because she hadn't heard whether or not she'd been accepted. She'd convinced herself she hadn't made the team.

"Oh boy do I remember. You applied for a spot on the Texas team, and you were all worried because you hadn't heard anything."

She'd been uptight about the sheer scope of the competition. If her team won, she could take home money and prizes not to mention a ton of scholarships. It had been all she could talk about.

"I remember," I said, "you could become famous and queen of the question-and-answer crowd. Your picture would be on TV, and there would be a parade in your honor . . . maybe, even your own hair spray line. Did I leave anything out?'"

"Okay, so, you do remember."

"I should. You only told me about it five thousand times. And I think Gus talked about it like seven or eight hundred more. You could say that, yes, I'm up to speed on the contest."

Over the miles of phone line, I could hear her smile.

"Well, you know I wanted so much to make the team . . ."

"I told you not to worry, remember?"

"I know, but I was worried anyway."

"And?"

"Well, I don't have to worry anymore. I got in! I made it!"

So that was her big news. I smiled, as Rachel shrieked into the phone, launching into some cheerleader-war-party-riding-down-the-hill-on-a-pinto-pony chant that almost damaged my ear drums.

"Aren't you happy for me? Isn't it the coolest? They only picked twenty-five students in the state and I made it. The letter was waiting for me when I got home. I'm on the team!"

I *was* happy. I knew it was a big deal to her. Besides, with everything she'd been though, and all the work she'd done in spite of all she'd been through, she deserved a break.

"You rock, baby. So when and where is the big competition?"

"Well, my most handsome boyfriend, that's the best part."

"What do you mean?"

"Alex you are not that dense. Clue in."

"Stop fooling around, Rachel, and just tell me."

"Okay, dork, the competition is October 19th—six weeks from today—and, you'll love this: It's at Oklahoma State University . . . in Stillwater."

This time, there was a lot more shouting, only this time it came from me.

# CHAPTER THIRTY-THREE

MY PARENTS MUST have heard the shouts, and it must have scared them, because they came flying up the stairs and into my room. Bill's eyes were about the size of plates, when he ripped open the door.

"Son...son, are you okay?"

"Heck, yeah," I said. That war-chant-thing was pretty cool, once you got the hang of it. I stopped, leaned over, and put my hands on my knees. "Sorry. Gotta catch my breath."

After I wheezed a few times (*where's Trevor and his inhaler when you needed them?*) I filled my parents in on what was going on.

"Rachel. It's Rachel," I said, still bouncing-off-the-wall happy. "She made the academic team, and the competition's going to be here at OSU!"

Bill and Clarise stood there like zombies. No words. No shouts. Nothing. Just strange faces as they exchanged looks.

"Don't you see? I get to see her again—soon. And you can meet her, too. Isn't this great? She's going to be here, in Stillwater."

More weird looks. What was wrong with these people? Didn't

they hear me? You'd think they'd had the news for weeks. I tried again. "Didn't you hear me? Rachel, she's coming here to Stillwater. In October. Just a few weeks away." I snapped my fingers. "Hello? Anybody home?"

I guess they figured they'd kept me waiting for their response too long, because just as I was ready to push them out of my room and head back to my closet, Bill broke out in this huge "guess-what-I-know-that-you-don't-know" grin.

"Isn't that great?" He was all smiles. He didn't say anything else, just stood there, smiling and looking stupid. It was Clarise's turn.

"That's wonderful honey. Did Rachel give you any of the details? When she'll be here? Things like that?"

I paused for a moment and thought back. Now I was a little confused. "Well, now that you mention it, she did say she already had her room booked. She just didn't say where."

Bill—still with the stupid, dorky smile—finally spoke: "She's not staying at a hotel, son."

It was my turn to look stupid. "Huh?"

"I said, 'she's not staying at a hotel.' Both the Holiday Inn and the Ramada are booked that week. So is the hotel on campus."

"But she was so excited. She's not staying in Stillwater?"

He laughed. The look on my face must have been a strange mix of weird, disappointment, and confusion. "I didn't say she wasn't staying in Stillwater. I just said she wasn't staying at any of the hotels here. And I know all this, because I listen first, then I ask questions."

I looked at Bill, then at Clarise, then back at Bill. What was he trying to say?

*Yes, crime stoppers, once again, it's Agent Alex, the world's foremost authority on—everything. And today, he has no idea what's going on. Stay tuned to next week's exciting episode of "Bill the Know-it-All!"*

I frowned. I focused on Bill who seemed to be the problem.

"You're not making any sense. What's going on?"

With that, he sat down on the bed in front of me. This time the smile on his face was happy, genuine. And I had the strangest feeling I was going to like what he had to say, too.

"Son, I'm sorry. I shouldn't have yanked your chain so hard. But I couldn't help it. I was telling the truth about the hotels. They are all booked because of the academic competition and OSU's homecoming. But when Rachel called back, your mother and I both talked to her and helped her find a place to stay."

*Yeah, I'm listening—get to the point Bill.*

"Well, okay. I mean, thanks, I guess." I gave a little nod. "That was nice of you guys."

Bill stuck his chest out like he's prone to do when he knows he's got it right. I wasn't sure it was quite deserved in this instance, but then, who was I to say?

"Yes, it was darn nice of us," he said. "It was about the nicest thing I've done for you since sending your moping, angry butt to that treatment center. Because the place we found for Rachel is here, with us."

> *Step right up. Step right up. See the amazing Alex actually pick his face up off the floor after his parents freak him out for the fourth time in one evening. Yessirree, folks, this look alone is worth the price of admission . . .*

"Are you serious?"

I was shocked. Never, in all my life, did I think my parents would be so cool.

"Yes. Yes, son, we are. We talked to Rachel, and her parents, and told them we'd be happy to let her stay with us. Jenny offered Rachel her room for the stay; so in October, when Rachel gets here, you'll get to see her every morning and every evening."

His smile filled the room.

Then he patted me on the arm.

"It was your mom's idea. She thought you'd like that."

For the first time in almost five years, I hugged my parents.

FOR THE NEXT few weeks, Rachel and I burned up the airwaves between Amarillo and Stillwater. I was happy about her upcoming visit, but the days dragged. October, would it never come?

Then football season started—without me on the team. I think my parents worried I'd revert back to Angry Boy. But while it was difficult knowing I wasn't going to play with my friends, I lived through it.

Coach Knott must have still been mad about how it had all gone down, because he cornered me one afternoon at school and told me that he wanted me back on the team. He said the team needed me. He said he was pretty sure I would be able to play my senior year.

I liked the sound of that.

Anyway, September finally bit the dust, and it was October. One day it was the fourth and then the next thing I knew, it was the six-teenth. I rushed around the house, trying to finish some last minute chores before Rachel arrived.

Her parents were bringing her. And, since my parents had in-vited them to stay the weekend, there was plenty to do. That Sat-urday I spent all day at the grocery store playing cart-pusher and sack-boy for Clarise, because she'd planned these huge, elaborate dinners—candles and, get this, wine—and her shopping list looked like it could wrap around the earth a couple of times.

Bill, being Mr. Hospitality, said he would grill the steaks for the first night. He might be a classical music geek, but the man could grill some serious beef. I figured if Rachel ate at my house like she ate at camp, he should come out looking like a major hero. Once her menus were finalized, Clarise moved her to-do list to the rest of the house. She bought new sheets and pillowcases, then she and Jenny gussied up the place from top to bottom.

Jenny didn't complain about the extra chores, either. Instead, she followed me around and asked questions about Rachel. At first it bugged me, but that changed the night before Rachel and her folks arrived in Stillwater. We'd just finished running the vacuum through the house for about the hundredth time when Jenny stopped, walked over, and threw her arms around me.

"I'm so glad you're back," she said. "I love you so much. I'm sorry if I make you mad, but I missed you and I don't ever want you to die. And, well, I'm glad you're better because I-love-you-bunches-and-I-just-really-missed-you-and-I-don't-ever-want-to-lose-you."

She blurted everything out in one breath, then held onto me like she was afraid to let go. I smiled, wrapped my arms around her, and kissed her on the cheek.

"Hey, Jenn? I'm glad I'm back, too. And I may tease you and stuff, but I missed you, too. I wouldn't want anyone else for my little sis. And, I love you bunches. And I promise I won't ever scare you like that again, okay?"

After that, it was downhill to the Clark family's arrival.

I didn't tell my parents or Jenny at the time, but I thought it was cool how hard they worked to get the place perfect for the Clarks. I knew they wanted to make Rachel and her folks feel okay about staying with us.

So, yeah, call me impressed.

Even after Bill tried—for the second time—to give me the ol' sex talk, everything between us was still okay. I dodged the encore chat by telling him that he had nothing to worry about. I swore to him I had no intention of trying to sneak down the hall to Rachel's room or anything else juvenile like that.

I don't think he believed me, but I was pretty sure he'd hoped that was what I would say.


FINALLY THE BIG DAY arrived. It was Friday. I bailed out of school early, raced home, and took the world's fastest shower. New jeans, nice shirt, and even socks.

Rachel and her folks were supposed to arrive at four-thirty.

They hit our neighborhood about three minutes late. Those extra three minutes felt like an eternity. I watched their car glide quietly down our street, then pull into our driveway. Everything was in slow motion. The car doors opened, and Rachel's parents got out first. They turned, and then the back door of the car flung open.

Rachel stepped out wearing snug fitting jeans and a yellow button-down shirt. She'd pulled her long hair up into a ponytail. Her eyes scanned the house, the yard, her parents, then my mom, then Jenny, then the dog, then Jenny's bike, then my father.

Then me.

When she saw me, she dropped her backpack and raced across the driveway. Her eyes sparkled as she jumped into my arms and wrapped herself around me like a beautiful, sweet willow tree. I held her and breathed deeply. She smelled so good—this time, spice and vanilla—I never wanted to let go.

Never had I felt anything so warm, so soft, so incredible. We twirled there on the driveway until finally she stepped back, looked me right in the eye, and nailed me with the slurpiest, sweetest, longest, yes-I'm-kissing-you-in-front-of-god-and-everyone, best tasting kiss I'd ever had.

Believe me, when I tell you it was worth the wait. It went on so long that I heard Rachel's dad go "hmmmuph" and cough and hack, trying to get our attention.

We didn't care. We kissed and kissed and kissed, while our families stood around us in a weird circle. Nobody said anything; nobody tried to pull us apart. And I give them credit for that.

When Rachel stepped away from me, I was dazed. Bill came to my rescue.

"Well, everyone," he said in his radio-announcer voice. "Now that we've all said 'hello,' let's all go in and have some iced tea."

I followed Rachel back to the trunk of her car, while her parents went with my parents and Jenny into the house. It took several more kisses before we made it inside with the rest of the bags, but once the door shut we started the most amazing week of our lives.

# CHAPTER THIRTY-FOUR

SURE AT FIRST, EVERYONE was formal and stiff with each other. But that was okay. We were basically a room full of strangers. Since Rachel and I were the only ones who knew each other, it was like being stuck in a nice hotel lobby with a bunch of people you'd just met. But, God love Bill, he aced the steaks—Rachel's dad (*remember, he's the other Bill*) raved about them, said it was the finest steak he'd ever had. Coming from a Texan, Bill said that was a serious compliment.

Clarise and Evelyn (*Rachel's mom*) bonded over washing dishes in the kitchen. I rolled my eyes when they started swapping kid stories. After dinner, Clarise brought out the wine, and the four of them sat around and drank and talked and laughed, and, as far as I could tell, had a great time.

Rachel spent lots of time with Jenny. They struck up a mutual admiration society that's sole purpose was to tease me. Before long, Jenny was ready to claim Rachel as the big sister she'd never had. As for me, I hung back, trying to play it cool. Basically I was waiting for the moment when I could have Rachel all to myself.

Eventually, Clarise clued in and sent Jenny off to bed. Then she suggested I take Rachel for a walk around the neighborhood, as she was sure "we had some catching up to do." I decided then and there that Clarise was much smarter than I'd ever guessed.

Rachel and I headed out to tour the neighborhood. We ended up on the swings at Emerson Elementary School, just down the road from my house. We talked some and kissed. Then we kissed a lot more and talked some. Then we talked some more and did some more kissing, then, finally, we kissed and talked.

"I didn't think I'd ever get here," she told me.

"Neither did I, but boy am I glad you're here now."

"At first I wasn't sure if my parents were going to let me stay at your house. They talked about it a lot, but I'm pretty sure they're okay with it now."

"Really?"

"Yeah. I overheard my dad tell my mom, that they 'had nothing to worry about,' and that your parents were 'good people.' "

"Well, at least they don't think we're a bunch of morons."

"Alex, you and your family are not morons. Why would you say that? Besides, after dad told mom how you defended me from Danny, she had to come and meet you. See, mom was the only one who saw Danny for what he was. She couldn't stand him from the beginning. I have never seen her dislike someone so much."

I had a new appreciation for Mrs. Clark.

"So she didn't like him either, huh?"

Rachel slugged me again.

"Noooo. Now be quiet. Right now, you are the White Knight in my mom's eyes, so enjoy it."

Rachel twirled a long strand of her hair.

"I guess I shouldn't make fun of her. I mean she was right. He was a jerk. Anyway enough about Danny, she also said you were handsome and a true hero, so there."

"Oh, great."

"What do you mean?"

"Well, doesn't the hero always die at the end of the movie?"

"Not this time."

Eventually we wandered back to my house, just as the second bottle of wine disappeared. Everyone started the "isn't it time for bed" routine, and my mom started handing out blankets, directing people to their rooms, and basically making sure everyone got tucked in okay.

I kissed Rachel good night and hit the rack. I laid there for an hour. A zillion thoughts raced through my head. Then, slowly, I started to crash. I hadn't been asleep long when I felt something soft touch my cheek.

"Alex, baby? Are you asleep?"

"Huh?" I rolled over to find Rachel silhouetted against the moonlight in a pair of sweats and a University of Texas T-shirt.

"I can't sleep. I didn't want to go to bed just yet."

"What time is it?"

"After midnight," she said. "Everyone else is asleep; I can tell by the snores."

I laughed. I slipped out of bed and put on my shorts and a shirt.

"What's wrong?" I asked. "Are you okay?"

"Yeah," she whispered. "I just wanted to talk to you some more."

"Okay. Come on. I know a great place."

I took her by the hand, and we slipped down the stairs to the utility room behind the kitchen.

"Follow me. You'll like this." I grabbed a small blanket off the dryer and opened the back door. We walked out onto the wooden deck overlooking the backyard. It was chilly, so I wrapped the blanket around both of us. There, framed against the big maple trees, a full moon hung low in a deep purple October sky. It looked like a million stars were out. I pointed to a spot just above the horizon.

"There, see that? That's the constellation of Orion, the hunter."

Rachel snuggled close to me.

"The stars are so bright here."

"Yeah, Kev and I used to camp out and stargaze all the time. We probably spent more time camping out than we did inside. He's the one who taught me all the planets and constellations."

I was getting ready to show Rachel the planet Mercury when she turned and kissed me again.

"Alex I want you to know how much I love you. I'm really, really in love with you. So bad it hurts sometimes. I know we're young, but I don't want to be with anyone else—ever. Just you."

Her kiss tasted like peaches. I knew I loved her, too. And I'd told her that before. But right now, she seemed scared. Her words had an edge to them, like this was something new.

"Rachel, you have to understand something. I'm not good at this. You're the first girl—other than Jenny and my mom—who's ever told me they loved me. Never mind the 'really, really' part."

I looked down at my feet.

"Rachel, you're also the first girl I've ever gotten so close to. It's just, well, it's hard to explain . . ."

Her body tensed.

"You mean, *you don't love me*?"

Okay, that wasn't what I expected. Man, I sucked at this boy-friend stuff. Please I prayed don't let her cry. I quickly pulled her next to me and wrapped my arms around her.

"No, no. What I was trying to say—and I'm sorry I suck so badly at it—is that you're the best thing that's ever happened to me. I don't want to be with anyone else, either. And Rachel, I *really, really, really* love you, too."

There, that came out better. She pushed herself back from me and looked deeply into my eyes.

"Do you mean that?"

"With every single *really*. Cross my heart. Since the first moment I saw you, I've had this feeling in my belly. I don't know how to explain it, but trust me it's there. It's a good, comforting feeling, like being under a warm blanket or listening to your favorite song. I only get it when I'm around you." I kissed her slow and soft. "And I never, ever want that feeling to go away."

That seemed to convince her. We didn't say much after that. We just stood there, holding each other, surrounded by a zillion stars, under a fat, round Oklahoma moon.

SATURDAY DAWNED CRISP, sunny, and amazing. Our family spent most of the day showing Rachel and her parents around Stillwater, including a quick cruise through campus so Rachel would know where the student union was on Monday. Then we headed over to Eskimo Joe's for a lunch of burgers and a monster plate of cheese fries, a Joe's specialty.

Clarise had planned another huge dinner at the house, so we cut the afternoon part of the tour short and headed back to Countryside Drive. Clarise said the recipe—it was Italian—was complicated, so she wanted to get an early start. Bill was doing dessert.

It was worth having to cut the town tour short. Clarise made this killer pasta dish she'd never cooked before—or so I thought at the time—and Bill baked what promised to be the best cheesecake ever to grace our dining room table.

"So please tell me again what you call this, Clarise?" Evelyn asked, as she spooned another bite into her mouth. "It's absolutely amazing."

"It's called *Bianca Verde*. I stole the recipe from a wonderful little restaurant in Tulsa. I never cook it, except," my mom glanced my way, "when the kids are gone. It's a special thing between Bill and me."

Rachel licked her spoon.

"The name means green and white. Doesn't it?"

My mom beamed. The girl loved her food *and* could translate; I could tell Rachel had already won a place in my mom's heart.

"Why yes, dear, it does. It's spinach tortellini with Italian sausage, sun-dried tomatoes, black olives, and a few other choice goodies."

Fifteen minutes later, mom was still talking about how she and dad used to go to this little hole-in-the-wall restaurant and eat this dish, and how the restaurant was going to be closed, and how when she and dad found out, they called the waiter over to their table and coaxed the recipe from him.

Rachel's mom threw back her head and gave a hearty laugh.

"What a wonderful story and a wonderful dish," she said. "Rachel, you may have to take the bus back to Texas alone. I think I'll stay here, though at the rate Bill and Clarise are feeding us I'll be waddling to my room."

Yes, so far, the weekend was a success. Rachel's folks liked my folks and my parents liked Rachel's folks. Jenny liked everyone, even me, so everything was just about perfect.

Of course, it couldn't stay that way.

# CHAPTER THIRTY-FIVE

NOW IT WASN'T LIKE the adults suddenly went mad or anything. And, at first, nobody except me caught on. Honestly, if it hadn't been for that extra strong cup of coffee I had and Rachel's mother having that third glass of wine, I don't think I would have figured the whole thing out.

We'd finished dinner, and Bill was carefully slicing up his mocha-flavored cheesecake. Rachel's mom had just poured herself another glass of wine, when she started going on and on about her little girl and how fast she'd grown up and how scared she'd been . . .

At first I was only about half-listening. Bill was shuttling plates of cheesecake back and forth from the kitchen to the dining room. Mom and Rachel's dad, the other Bill, had left earth for Planet Merlot. I don't know if anyone was actually paying attention to what Mrs. Clark was saying. But then something told me to dial in.

"Anyway, I just about came unglued when we all found out that Rachel was going to have heart surgery again," Evelyn said. "It was devastating. We had tried so hard to make sure she had a normal life, but that, that was the most difficult thing we'd ever faced."

Rachel put her hand on her mother's arm.

"But, Mom, I'm fine now. Doctor Evans said I'm fine, and I'm not taking nearly as many pills as I did last year."

"I know, honey, but it was just so frightening. I don't know what I'd do if I lost you."

Bill reached for his wife's hand.

"It's okay, Evelyn; she's doing wonderful, and her new heart is rock solid."

"Yeah, Mom, I promise—I feel great."

Evelyn took another sip of her wine. I could tell their words hadn't quieted her fears.

"You won't understand," she said to her daughter, "until you're grown. The fear, just the incredible fear."

I watched Rachel's expression change.

"I was scared, too, Mom. *Really* scared."

Her mother continued on as if she hadn't heard her.

"The waiting and the not knowing. And it took forever to find a donor. It dragged on and on. They thought they'd found one, then it fell through. You had hope one minute only to have it dashed the next."

Rachel smiled a weak, watery smile.

"But the day Doctor Evans called was a happy day, wasn't it?"

"Yes, honey, it was. But it was a sad day for some other family. Don't you remember how long everything took? That flight from B'nai Tulsa, the one that carried your new heart? We thought it would never arrive. What a nightmare."

About then the wine ran out. As Evelyn reminisced, Clarise tried to comfort her, and the two Bills alternated between fun guy talk to let's get the tipsy lady to bed.

We moved outside on the back porch and watched the sun fade. Then everyone drifted back into the house. Clarise, Rachel, and Jenny put the dishes up, and the Bills slipped off to watch a football game. I was at loose ends, trying to process what I'd heard.

When Rachel joined me, I could tell she was worried about being ready for the academic bowl on Monday, so after a quick break on the deck we spent the rest of Saturday prepping her for the competition. By the time the local news anchor signed off, everyone was wiped out, and we all stumbled off to bed.


ON SUNDAY, WE EXCHANGED about a million "good-byes" and "please come backs," then we all stood on the lawn and watched Rachel's parents drive off into the afternoon sun. That evening, we dined on leftovers—dinner was more pasta and a huge salad—and I helped Rachel study some more for the competition. After three solid hours of question after question, I was pretty sure she could have taken on the boys from *Encyclopedia Britannica*.

Since Rachel had to be at the university early Monday, I offered to drive her to campus. My mom had—yes, she'd surprised me yet again —loaned me her car for the week, so I could chauffeur Rachel back and forth to the competition. If mom needed something, she just sent Rachel and me to the store.

Funny, those trips always took a long time.

Anyway come Monday morning, I dropped Rachel off at OSU, then hit Stillwater High in time for my first class. It was a typical school day, and the only time I came close to losing it was when I walked past Kev's old locker. At first I didn't notice it, but some kid bumped into me and the next thing I knew, I was looking right at number five-two-one. They say time travel doesn't exist except in books and movies, but they're wrong. In that moment, I was back to the week after Kev's death, helping the principal pack up his things.

Determined not to go back to Angry Boy, I shook off the memories and headed to history. It helped that we were having an exam in that class—nothing like an essay question to distract you. I did a lot better on the test than I thought I would, so I was in a good mood when I picked Rachel up after school.

She, on the other hand, looked hammered. The elimination rounds had started, and I guess it was intense. It had taken a lot out of her, but Rachel had nailed the first round, and now she was on to the second level of competition. Still she was worried.

"I need you to help me study some more, tonight. Okay?"

"Sure. Hey, I think it's helping me, too. I got a B-plus on my history exam."

"Awesome. I knew there were some brains beneath that great tan."

I prepared myself for another night of academic Q&A.

"ALEX? ALEX! ALEX, please wake up." Something or someone was shaking me, and I swore before I bothered to open my eyes that it had better not be Jenny. I stretched. The couch felt great. It had been a long time since I had crashed in the living room.

"What? Hey, stop it! I'm awake."

"Honey, it's me, Rachel. Sorry, but we both fell asleep. I can't study anymore. I'm going to bed."

I rubbed my face, sat up, and looked at her.

"Sorry. Okay. I'm beat, too. Same time tomorrow?"

"Oh yeah. I love you, my hunky, study buddy."

Maybe there was something to this school stuff.

I DON'T KNOW WHY, but I couldn't get back to sleep after Rachel went upstairs. I tossed and turned for another hour. You'd think after taking a test of my own, studying with Rachel, and doing everything else, I'd have been out like a light. But there I was. Three in the morning and I was as wide awake as I've ever been. Go figure.

Looking back, it was just plain weird. The past few days kept running through my head like a DVD on repeat. I kept seeing the same images and hearing the same stuff. But it was in pieces, like someone had done a poor editing job and spliced several scenes from different movies together. I relived Rachel's kiss in the driveway and my father's jokes. I saw my mom's worried smile, and the night Danny tried to rape Rachel. I saw last weekend when Rachel's mom talked about how scared she was when it came time for Rachel's heart transplant.

What was it Mrs. Clark had said? Something about a flight from Tulsa? What was the name of that hospital. Tulsa-something? With a V? Or a B? I glanced at the clock. Ugh. At this rate, I'd get four hours sleep tops.

I had to get some shut-eye. I grabbed another blanket, turned the fan on my face, and pushed myself down in the bed. B'nai Tulsa. That was the name. Now why did I care?

BY THE TIME WEDNESDAY ROLLED AROUND, Rachel was sitting pretty. The Texans hammered some team from Norman North, then went on to crush the teams from Lawton and Anadarko and North Tulsa. Because her team had fared so well Tuesday, it didn't have to compete again until late Thursday afternoon. There wasn't much going on at school, so I'd planned to skip Thursday and hang out with my favorite Texas beauty. At least that was my plan Wednesday afternoon.

By six, we'd put away a large pizza and enough iced tea to fill a swimming pool. Though she didn't need to, Rachel had wanted to study some more, so we'd hit the books until the news came on, then headed back out to the deck.

We'd had our first frost the night before, and Wednesday night arrived with a cold, rainy mist. We didn't stay out on the deck long. Instead Bill built a fire, so we could all hang out in the living room, then my parents crashed for the evening. Jenny was off at a friend's house—her class was going on a field trip the next day—so it was just Rachel and me.

We caught up on our kissing and talking, and about midnight she started to yawn. I was pretty sure the evening was over. I walked her to Jenny's room, kissed her good night, and headed to my own room—my mind overflowing with the names of seventeenth-century French poets and images of Rachel in pink sweats.

Sleep came quickly, but it didn't last. About three in the morning I sat straight up in bed, wide awake. To this day, I can't explain how I figured it all out, but trust me it was like the little guy in my head turned on the light switch and then pointed at the answer on the chalkboard. Suddenly it was that clear—and I understood everything. All these weird feelings, all those images. Now I knew why. I got it. I started to sweat. My pulse raced.

"Oh man," I said to myself. "Everything fits."

I threw on jeans, a hoodie, shoes but no socks. I rushed to my closet and reached back inside to the shelf where my sweaters were stashed. Next to the gray wool one, sat a box of stuff—useless stuff, mostly—but stuff I couldn't seem to throw away. Inside, on the top of the box, was an orange folder, Kev's report. I'd kept it the day I helped Mrs. Howerton clean out his locker.

I grabbed the folder, shut the closet door, and turned on the lamp by my bed. My eyes raced back and forth across the pages. Funny, I'd never read this stuff—I'd only heard it secondhand from Kev—and I'd never paid much attention then. When I finished reading, I slipped down the hall to Jenny's room. The door was unlocked, and there, curled up under a big blue quilt, was Rachel. My hands were sweaty; I felt myself shake. I tapped her shoulder and whispered. "Rachel, Rachel baby?"

She moaned softly and rolled onto her other side. I knelt by the bed and whispered in her ear again.

"Rachel, it's me, Alex. Wake up."

"Huh, Alex? What's wrong? I need to sleep."

"I'm sorry, Rach, but I've got to talk to you," I said. "Get up. It's important. We have to talk."

She must have heard something in my voice, because she woke up immediately.

"Is something wrong? You look weird."

"Come on. Get dressed. Please, this is important?"

Now Rachel looked concerned.

"Okay, give me just a sec."

I watched her slip a T-shirt over her sweatpants. I grabbed her sweatshirt and handed it to her.

"Dress warm, okay?"

I could tell I'd frightened her, but it couldn't be helped. I didn't have time to explain; she'd have too many questions. No, this had to be done now. Right now. It explained everything.

"Okay, now what?"

I motioned her to follow me, and we slipped downstairs, out the back door, and into the frosty night air.

"Alex, what are you doing? Where are you taking me? What's wrong? What's that you're holding?"

With each question, her voice shook a little more. Stay with me Rachel, I thought to myself, it'll all make sense soon.

"You have to trust me, Rachel. I promise it's nothing bad, okay? But you have to trust me. Please? I just figured everything out. It all makes sense now."

"Okay," said Rachel. "It's just, you're so intense."

"I know, just trust me, okay?"

With that, we started down the street.


THE HOUSE WAS ONLY three blocks away. And the dark didn't matter. I could have walked there blindfolded. Down Countryside, over to Baycliff, and then left, down Rising Oak. There, the fourth house on the right, yellow shutters, two stories, big fireplace. Rachel shivered as we walked up to the door.

"Alex, you do know it's four in the morning? What are you do-ing?"

She said "doing" just as I started to pound on the door. When I didn't stop, she tried to grab my fist.

"Alex! Alex, stop! You'll wake up whoever lives here. Stop!"

I didn't even hesitate.

I just let my fist fly, pounding on the door, like my life depended on it.

"Alex!"

Rachel was frantic now. I knew she was scared someone would come to the door with a shotgun, but it wasn't like that. In a minute she'd understand.

"Alex, let's go. It's way too early. You're not thinking . . ."

She never finished the sentence. In the middle of her pleading, the door opened. A stream of bright yellow light flooded the porch, pushing back the wet, cold night. There, in front of me, stood a man I hadn't talked to in almost a year. He was in shorts and a blue sweatshirt. He was sleepy, and, at first, he didn't recognize me.

"Yes, can I help you?"

I stopped shaking. I stepped into the light.

"Mr. Rubenstein, it's me, Alex. I need to talk to you."

# CHAPTER THIRTY-SIX

NEIL RUBENSTEIN LOOKED as if he'd seen a ghost. His eyes went wide, and he didn't say anything for a couple of minutes. Rachel and I stood there waiting for him to make a decision. Would he let us in? Rachel squeezed my hand, reassuringly. "Why, Alex," he said, after getting his bearings. "I'm glad to see you. It's been a long, long time."

"I'm sorry to bother you, sir, and I know it's late, but this couldn't wait. It's a matter of life and death. Please will you let us in?"

Mr. Rubenstein nodded and stepped aside. Rachel and I walked into Kev's house then stood by the front door, near the staircase.

"I need to ask you some questions. I know how weird they're going to sound to you, but I need your help. I'm running out of time. I think I figured the whole thing out. If you wouldn't mind…"

Before Mr. Rubenstein could respond, Kev's mom, Anne, and his sister, Erin, appeared out of the darkness.

"Neil? Neil, who is it? What's wrong?"

"It's okay honey. Everything's fine," Mr. Rubenstein said over his shoulder.

"Who was banging on the door?"

Long pause. I could tell it was awkward for Mr. Rubenstein, so I cut him some slack. Besides, I was the one interrupting his sleep.

"It's me, Mrs. Rubenstein, Alex. Alex Anderson."

I could hear Erin and her mother whispering back and forth. I was sure they both had several billion questions starting with, "What the hell is he doing here?" But I didn't have time. Not now.

"I need to talk with you and your husband, ma'am. Please?"

I held my breath. I heard her hesitate for a moment, and then a sigh of resignation.

"Well, okay . . . yes, come in."

Kev's parents ushered us into the kitchen to a large square table. Rachel sat next to me. Up until then, I don't think either of them realized Rachel was with me, because as he turned around, Kev's dad did this double take, and he stopped.

"Ah, Alex, are you going to introduce us to your friend?"

"Sure sir, this is Rachel. Rachel Clark. We met this summer."

By this time, Mrs. Rubenstein had started coffee, and everybody was about as awake as they were going to get this early in the morning. It's amazing how quickly you wake up when the kid that killed your son is sitting in your living room with a girl you've never met.

Mr. Rubenstein poured a cup of coffee and sat down. "So, what is it that's so urgent? What do you need to talk to us about right now, Alex?"

I had expected this to be strange, and I was right. It was. But, I had no other choice. So I just started talking and prayed that some of it would make sense.

"I wanted to talk to you about the day Kev, well, the day Kev died. I have some questions."

Suddenly it got real quiet. Mr. Rubenstein set down his coffee.

"But Alex, you were there. You were at the hospital long before Anne and I got there. What else do you need to know? I mean other than what I said that day."

"It's not that, sir. And, honestly, I didn't come here for a fight.

Actually, just the opposite. Please don't think that I'm still upset about that."

Underneath the table, I squeezed Rachel's hand. "What I need to know is what happened after my mom, Jenny, and I left the hospital that night. That's what I wanted to ask you about."

With that, Mr. Rubenstein picked up his cup and took a big gulp of coffee. I watched his expression fade from scowl to something softer. Now I was looking at the man I remembered.

"Well, there's not that much to tell," he said. "After you and your family left, we stayed and spoke with the doctor. It was very difficult."

I knew the memories about that night had flooded back to him. I needed to make this quick.

"What happened to Kev after that?"

Mr. Rubenstein took another sip of coffee.

"I stayed with him. After the doctors finished, they cleaned him up as much as possible, and I sat in the operating room with him until the man from the funeral home came. Then after they took him away, Anne and I drove home. It was the longest drive of our lives."

Across the room, Erin sniffled. Her mother pulled her close, then looked at me, puzzled and as if she was angry.

"Alex, I don't understand. I remember how close you were to Kevin, and, honestly, I considered you one of my own kids, but we haven't seen you in a long, long time—not since Kevin died. We tried to talk with you. We wrote. We called, but nothing. We knew you were hurting. We understood that," said Mrs. Rubenstein. "But you never stopped to consider how we felt. You didn't even speak to us at Kevin's funeral.

"Now suddenly, you show up at four in the morning with a young woman we don't know, wanting us to relive the day our son died. Please help me understand what's going on."

I looked at the floor. It had all made so much sense in the comfort of my own home. Now I was having second thoughts. I thought I had figured everything out, but what if I was wrong. I knew Rachel felt awkward, but I hadn't stopped to consider how Kev's mom and dad would feel. What was I doing here?

*Yes, crime stoppers this is the new game show, "I'm a Total Moron," starring your favorite low-life, Alex Anderson...*

"I'm sorry, Mrs. Rubenstein. But, honestly, I felt so guilty about Kev and that night. What Mr. Rubenstein said, stuck in my head. For the past year, I've been so messed up that I spent the summer getting therapy, but, I swear, I'm better now. Not a day goes by that I don't think about my best friend. Kev was the brother I never had.

"I loved him and I miss him something awful."

The words weren't out of my mouth, before Anne Rubenstein got up, stepped over, and pulled me out of my chair and into a warm embrace.

"Alex, honey, we know. We miss him, too. And you. You two were such a part of our lives. Kevin's death caused such a huge wound, one that will never heal. And when we lost you, too, well, that was almost as bad. It was almost like losing a second son."

Kev's mom pulled me closer.

"I know Neil said some horrible things to you that night, things that he regrets to this day. But please, you have to believe us when we tell you that it wasn't your fault. We know that. It was a drunk driver, an accident. We know you loved Kev. You protected him when no one else would. You were his best friend in the whole world."

Kev's dad stood and put his arm around me.

"Alex, I've owed you an apology for that night for a long time. I'm so sorry. I can't explain why I said what I said at the hospital; there is no excuse for it. But try to understand.

"One minute I was at work, trying to finalize a budget; the next, I'm standing in the emergency room, being told my son is dead. It was more than I could handle and I fell apart, but please know that I've regretted what I said to you every single day since then."

Now I was the one who felt guilty. This wasn't what I had meant to happen. I wasn't looking for true confessions. I needed information. Though if I was being honest with myself, Mr. Rubenstein's apology did make me feel better. And I think it made the rest of our conversation easier. Kev's mom let me go, and I tried to pick up where I'd left off.

"I believe you, sir. I swear I do. I didn't understand for a long time, but then Rachel explained it all to me. So please, it's okay. But, honestly, that's not what I wanted to talk to you about."

Kev's parents looked shaken. They didn't understand.

"Well, if that's not what you wanted to talk about, what is it?"

"Before he died, Kev told me he wanted to be an organ donor. Was that true?"

Neil Rubenstein looked at me like I'd lost my mind. I thought he might yell at me again, but on a night this strange what was the point? Instead, he attempted a smile, a weak, exhausted smile. I knew he thought I was crazy.

"Well, yes, it is. He talked to Anne and I about it and even enlisted Rabbi Goldberg's support. But I don't understand. How is that important?"

"Could you tell me what organs, he. . . he shared?"

It was the most personal question I'd ever asked another human being, and it bordered on being completely insensitive. To this day, I don't know how I managed to get the question out. But I had no choice.

Before her husband could answer, Kev's mom walked over to a small desk in the kitchen and opened the bottom drawer. She rustled through papers for a minute or two, then brought out a leather notebook. She laid the notebook on the table in front of me.

"It's all there," she said, in a matter-of-fact voice. "After Kevin was pronounced dead, the hospital, with our approval, contacted the organ network."

There was a long, silent pause in the room. I downed a big slug of coffee and looked at Kev's parents. His mom continued.

"Shortly after that, we signed a document, and Kevin's organs were harvested. He gave his organs to the TriState Organ Bank."

She turned a few pages over, until she found the one she wanted.

"He gave both corneas, his liver, and his kidneys."

She paused. And in that moment of silence, my heart dropped. Damn, I had been so sure, especially after reading his notebook.

"Was there anything else?"

"Oh yes, and . . . and his heart. He donated his heart, but that donation was the most difficult."

"Do you know anything about the people who . . ."

My half-asked question hung in the air.

"Very little," she said. "The network has strict rules about confidentiality, and it takes the consent of all those involved to release information. All we know is that a man in Arkansas received his corneas, and a boy, here in Oklahoma, was given his liver."

"Do you know anything about them?"

"Not much. As I said, there's so much paperwork involved. No one contacted us about those."

I took a deep breath.

"What about his . . . heart? Do you know who received it?"

Anne Rubenstein shook her head.

"No. That donation was probably the most painful for us to do. Originally, we were told a match had been found, but the flow of information stopped, and we never heard anything else."

Kev's mom patted the notebook in front of me.

"It's all here. I kept all the paperwork, the forms, and the letters. I don't know why, but I just couldn't bring myself to throw them away."

I slipped Kev's folder under the notebook. I wasn't sure I wanted the Rubensteins to know I had it just yet. So far, this wasn't going the way I'd envisioned it. It was one dead end after another. I had been so sure.

"Could you tell me when they did the operations?"

My question hit a wall. Mr. Rubenstein looked like he was in pain. I knew this wasn't what he wanted to relive much less talk about, but I needed to understand. I needed to know, and they did, too, though they didn't know it right now.

"Well, the organs were 'harvested'—that's the term they used—here in Stillwater," he said. "Then the organs and Kevin were flown to Tulsa. The funeral home worked with the organ network before his body was prepared for burial."

Mrs. Rubenstein pulled the notebook back across the table and thumbed through the pages. "It was at Tulsa B'nai B'rith," she said. "Rabbi Levenson helped us with arranging everything."

I reached towards her. "Could I see that again?"

Mrs. Rubenstein slid the notebook back to me.

"As you can see, the documents tell you what organ was taken but nothing else. Each organ is tested, typed, and cross matched for a donor, but they have to be harvested—oh I hate that word—quickly. Within hours."

I pointed to a yellow form with about a million numbers and all sorts of legal mumbo jumbo on it.

"What's this?"

"Neil was given that by a friend at the hospital. We weren't supposed to see it, but he knew someone who made us a copy. This is the donor network's tracking form. Each organ is assigned a unique number to make sure it goes where it's supposed to go. I believe they corresponded with the receiving hospital and the patient receiving the organ."

I pulled out the paper and folder.

Next to each different tracking number, was Kev's name, some personal information, and the organ he donated. Next to each organ was a number. I skimmed past the first entries. Nothing. I slipped Kev's school report on top of the folder. I opened it, and there on the third page was an interview with Rabbi Eugene Levenson from the B'nai B'rith hospital.

"Tulsa B'nai," I said. "I thought so."

The Rubensteins sat there with blank looks on their faces. I waved the paper at Rachel. She looked just as confused as to where I was going with all this. I said it again. And this time, I looked right at Rachel.

"Don't you see? Tulsa B'nai."

Rachel turned toward me with wonder in her eyes.

"Did you say Tulsa B'nai?"

"Yeah, I did. Isn't that the hospital that you used?"

Slowly, Rachel began to understand.

"Yeah, yeah it was."

She grabbed the report out of my hand.

"Let me see those."

Her eyes danced across each page.

"Oh my gosh, Alex. It's the same hospital. You don't think?"

I smiled. Yes, I did think. It's what had driven me to pull all these people from their warm beds on this cold, autumn morning.

"That's what I wanted to tell you. Now you see why I was in such a hurry."

Neil Rubenstein stepped in to calm things down.

"Alex, I'm not sure what you're driving at, but please remember that Tulsa B'nai is the main transplant center for the TriState Organ bank. Organs go from there to all parts of the country. It wouldn't surprise me if there were dozens of transplants made that same day Kevin died."

I understood his logic, but I was sure he was wrong. I just knew, like I knew I loved Rachel, like I knew no friend could ever replace my first and best friend, that I was right about this.

I looked back at the forms from the organ donor network. There, on the last page was the listing for Kev's heart. It had all sorts of information and one long tracking number:

*1XHT16OK-102080-BX5-3HDM.*

I picked up the folder again, and a small piece of paper fluttered to the table. It was a ripped piece off a sticky note; it must have been stuck on the back of one of the forms. It looked as if it was supposed to be a note, but it was more like code.

Someone had scribbled "TXF-15" across it in pen.

I handed the note to Mr. Rubenstein.

"Could you tell me what this means?"

"Oh, I'd forgotten about that," he said. "Last year I was in Tulsa on business. I had promised Anne I'd drop a donation off to the hospital foundation on my way out of town. While I was there, I bumped into Kevin's doctor. He said he'd had some information about the recipient of Kevin's heart.

"He said the heart had been used, but he couldn't remember the details. Anyway, he handed me that note, but as I went to ask him what it meant, he was paged, and we didn't get to finish our conversation. Since then, he and his family have moved to Minnesota. I never followed up on it. After all this time, it's probably not important."

Great. Another dead end. And I'd been so sure. Could I have screwed anything up worse? Guess it was time to exit, stage left. I touched Rachel's hand to signal we should go.

"I guess it's time for us to go. We've kept you up long enough." I looked at the Rubensteins. "I'm so sorry about getting you up in the middle of the night. Honestly, I was just so sure . . ."

I felt a tug on my sleeve.

"Alex. Wait. Wait just a sec."

Rachel had grabbed the forms I'd been looking at from the organ donation network and was frantically reading.

"Could you give me that list," she asked, "the one with the tracking numbers."

I shuffled through the pile of forms on the table and found the one that listed all the organs and numbers.

Rachel's hand trembled as she turned to the last page.

"Oh my God," she gasped.

## CHAPTER THIRTY-SEVEN

RACHEL READ FOR A FEW seconds more, and then it was like someone had flipped a switch on inside her. She looked up and she started yelling. Loud. Real loud.

"Oh my gosh! It's true! It's true! Oh my gosh! It's true!"

For a moment I thought she'd gone and lost her mind, but then I realized she must have seen something on the form that I hadn't seen.

"What?" I asked. "What is it?"

Rachel's hand trembled as she pointed to the paper.

"That number, see? It's the number. It's *my* number."

A FEW MINUTES LATER she had calmed down enough to try and explain what she had found to the rest of us, but she was still pretty excited. She kept shaking the paper in front of my face.

"Okay, this number proves it," she said. "It's true. It's the same number. You're right. You figured it out. It's the same number."

"The same as what?"

"It's the same number as the tracking number for my heart."

It was at that moment that Neil Rubenstein dropped one of his best coffee mugs. He leaned across the table, oblivious to the cracked mug and spilled coffee on the floor.

"Your heart? What are you talking about? *Your heart?*"

"I'm sorry. When Alex brought me here, I didn't know what he wanted. I didn't understand. I do now. See, last year I had a heart transplant. And the donor heart came from the Texas-Oklahoma region. My heart was shipped from Tulsa B'nai Hospital."

Neil Rubenstein smiled. I could tell he followed Rachel's logic, but he remained skeptical.

"But like I said before," he said, "hundreds of organ transplants are done at Tulsa B'nai."

This time, it was Rachel's turn to smile.

"But not with this number."

Kev's dad shook his head.

"How do you know that? How do you know that's the tracking number for your heart?"

Rachel pointed to her wrist.

"Because of my bracelet."

Her wrist was bare. Mr. Rubenstein looked more confused than ever, if that was possible.

Rachel gave him a huge smile.

"The night before my surgery, my grandmother gave me a sterling silver bracelet with a single heart charm. Engraved on the back of the heart was a message from her. It said she loved me. Engraved on the front was this big, long number."

Rachel pointed to the paper.

"That number."

It was Anne Rubenstein's turn to be shocked.

"But how can you be sure? How could you remember so long a number?"

"Ask me." Rachel said. "Before it was broken and lost this summer, I'd looked at that number about a million times a day. My grandmother said that bracelet represented two very special people in the universe who loved me: Her and the person who gave me my heart."

Rachel placed the form in front of Kev's father, then took him by the hand, looked him right in the eye, and said:

"Mr. Rubenstein that number is 1-X-H-T-1-6-O-K dash 1-0-2-0-8-0 dash B-X-5 dash 3-H-D-M."

She didn't even glance at the paper. "I've had that number memorized since the day of my operation."

Neil Rubenstein's face looked like he'd been jolted with about five hundred million volts of electricity.

"But, I don't . . ."

Rachel patted his hand.

"Don't you see? Kev gave his heart to me."


IN ALL MY LIFE, I'll never forget that morning, watching Rachel, watching the Rubensteins, watching everyone come to the same realization. It was almost too much to take in. Everyone sat there stone silent for several minutes. Then, since I figured I'd caused all this chaos, I figured I'd better do something to end it.

So I stood up and took Rachel's hand in mine.

Then I turned to the Rubensteins.

"Mr. and Mrs. Rubenstein, this is Rachel Lynn Clark. She's my girlfriend. She's the love of my life. In fact, she saved my life. She's wonderful, and beautiful, and sweet, and smart. She always smells good, and beating inside her is your son's, my best friend's, heart.

"Rachel has Kevin's heart."

# CHAPTER THIRTY-EIGHT

FIRST THERE WAS SILENCE. Then there was screaming—
lots and lots of screaming. But it was a joyful noise this time.
And then everyone exploded in his own way. Now this was
more like the reunion I'd had in mind. I had to bite my lip to keep
from grinning like a fool.

Erin screamed, "Oh my gosh," and Kev's dad just stood there
yelling, "Oh my, oh my" over and over. Anne Rubenstein dropped
her coffee mug (now I owed them two)—and it, too, shattered into
a million pieces on the floor. Not that anyone noticed.

Rachel stood there like a stone; her face soaked with tears. Erin
and her mother rushed to her side, grabbed my sweet girlfriend, and
held her like they were never going to let her go.

After giving them a little time together, Kev's dad came over and
gently pulled them apart. He reached for Rachel's face softly, like he
would a baby's.

Then he looked directly into her eyes and spoke.

It was almost a whisper:

"You mean, you have my Kevin's heart?"

Rachel nodded, as she took his hand and placed it over her scar. She pointed to the torn sticky note. "That note means 'Texas, fifteen-year-old female'—I'm sure of it. That was me. I was fifteen when I had my transplant."

I smiled and put my arm around Rachel.

"And, if you can't tell, she's pretty much all girl," I said.

*Yes, friends, in America right now, there are five thousand comedians starving, and Alex is performing for free.*

Mr. Rubenstein pulled his wife and daughter close, and then he turned to face Rachel and me.

"I don't know what to say. I'm speechless."

I knew what he meant. I couldn't help thinking it was a good thing we hadn't planned anything for the morning. As the shock of the discovery faded, everyone sat back down at the table. Rachel moved over between the Rubensteins and began to tell them her whole life's story.

When she got to this summer, she didn't hold back—even when it came to Danny and the attack. I could see they were shocked by Danny's cruelty and amazed by the resilience of the young woman sitting between them.

Every now and then, Rachel paused to take a breath, and I filled in the gaps about what had happened to me—from why I had been sent to the center to how Rachel and I met. When I told them about the gun in the paper sack, Neil Rubenstein grabbed my hand.

"Alex, again, I am so sorry. I never meant to hurt you; I don't know what we would have done if we had lost you, too."

We talked until sunrise, at which time Kev's mom and Erin took a break to show Rachel around their house. There were about a million photos of Kev for her to see—many with me in them, too. I blew off school and Kev's parents took off work. Around noon, we broke things up, because I had to have Rachel back on campus for Thursday's competition. We both promised the Rubensteins we'd come back soon and answer all the rest of their questions. After a billion hugs and lots more tears, Rachel and I stepped outside into the bright fall afternoon. I stole a kiss as we walked back home.

"You know, it felt good to be back at Kev's house," I said. "It has been so long. And, I can't remember the last time I actually saw Kev's mom smile."

Rachel squeezed my hand. "I still can't believe that you figured it all out. I am amazed. I knew we had a connection, a bond, but I never believed it had anything to do with my heart."

"Love has everything to do with your heart, silly."

It was my turn, just for once, to be the smart one.


THAT NIGHT THE RUBENSTEINS joined my family and Rachel's parents—who had set a land speed record driving in from Texas after we called them—to watch Rachel compete. She had the biggest cheering section in the competition. And though her team finished second, she still won tons of prizes and a big scholarship.

We all whistled and cheered and stomped, and generally made idiots of ourselves.

I could tell Rachel loved all our silliness.

The next day, we had all the families over, and we told them the entire story—the good, the bad, and the ugly. When I described the events that followed Rachel's attack at the hospital with the police, the Bills and Neil Rubenstein were ready to thump Mr. Redding and Rick—not to mention the police, but Rachel and I assured them we'd already taken care of the problem.

The next day, as Rachel and her folks were getting ready to leave, Rachel told me it had been the best trip of her entire life—not because of the competition but because of all she had learned about herself, about me, about Kev.

"Now I understand why I always feel safe around you," she said. "Why you were always there when I needed you, without me even asking or calling." She kissed me slow and soft. "And I know what you mean about the snakes, too. It's weird, but I feel both happy and sad. Sad because the Rubensteins lost their son and they loved him so much. Happy, because their son saved my life. But then I'm sad, because they are, and because you are, but then I'm happy again, because you all seem happier than you were. Does any of that make sense?"

I was actually a little dizzy from my head bobbing up and down in agreement. "Yeah, I think so. Just promise me you won't make me repeat it."

I pulled her against me.

"Right now, at this very moment, I feel like a huge weight has been lifted off my chest. And I'm not so sad about Kev anymore, because part of him is still alive. And, well, it's weird, too, because, I think there's more to the whole life-thing than just a piece of flesh being put into another person's body. There's an honest-to-god connection. Sort of supernatural. And in your case, I don't think it just happened by accident."

"I liked what Mr. Rubenstein told me the other night," Rachel said. "Remember?"

I was caught. I didn't remember. So much had been said that it was impossible to remember it all.

"He said a lot of stuff."

"Doofus. Remember? He told me that I didn't steal Kevin's heart, but that Kevin gave it to me. He said I stole your heart, but Kev's heart was his gift to me, a blessing from God."

I laughed.

"You were just like me; you tried to keep your scars hidden. But it didn't work. I discovered your scars and you found mine. Maybe we're not supposed to keep our scars hidden. Maybe it doesn't work that way. Maybe God expects you to have scars—and to share what you learn from them with others, and in doing so our weaknesses can become our strengths."

Rachel smiled. She put her hands on my shoulders and turned me towards her.

"You know, Alex, you do have an amazing family."

I laughed. "Yeah, Bill and Clarise are all right."

Rachel scowled at me.

"Why do you call them that?"

"Huh?"

"Why do you call them by their first names? They are your mom and dad."

I looked at my feet, not sure where she was going with this.

"Well, yeah, I know that. But it seems like I've called them Bill and Clarise forever."

"Forever?" Rachel looked doubtful.

"Well, ever since the accident—seems like forever."

Rachel shook her head. "Parents aren't perfect, Alex. They are just like the rest of us, but ever since the accident you've been putting distance between yourself and them."

I rolled my eyes.

"They don't care. They're used to it."

"No, they're not," Rachel said. "Ask them. And, yeah, I'll give you that your mom is a little goofy, but when things got tough for you they did everything they could to help you. They were there for you and you didn't even realize it.

"Sending you away was probably the hardest thing they ever did as parents, but they did it so they could have you back.

"They care about you and they love you.

"They are your mom and dad."

Now I felt bad. Rachel was making sense, and, well, I guess I'd never thought about it that way. The accident had blinded me to more than even I realized.

"Okay, okay, I see your point."

Rachel smiled. "Good. I feel better."

We walked across the lawn and opened the back door of my house. I glanced at her.

"You know, calling them Mom and Dad again will totally freak them out."

Rachel laughed and flung an arm around me.

"Sure it will—that's what makes it fun. But they'll also know they have their son back, and that will make them smile. Trust me."

"Okay. Okay. I said I would."

Rachel stopped me in the hall, ran her fingers through my hair, then kissed me.

"For a tanned, football-playing freak who went crazy for a while, you're pretty smart," she said.

"And you, my sweet girlfriend, are amazing. If you're not stealing hearts you're helping fix broken ones."

# EPILOGUE

SO THAT'S THE ENTIRE story. Heck, it even made my therapist cry. I had this great friend, I watched him die, and I freaked out over it. I even planned to kill myself. Then my folks sent me away, and I met the one girl who could make me feel better—the girl who would have died had she not been given the heart of my best friend.

Weird huh?

I will say right now that I firmly believe there's stuff in the world you can't explain. And, I also believe there's a God. And I don't think it matters what you call him, he's still God. And he has a connection with all of us.

So, you're wanting to know what happened next, right?

Well, Rachel went back to Texas, and it wasn't until about a month later at Thanksgiving that I saw her again. She and her family came to Stillwater, and our holiday dinner, trust me, was huge. The Rubensteins wanted us all to come to their house—my family, Rachel's parents, and her sisters. There were tons of people and it was great. The dads did all the cooking—most of us hate turkey, so we had steaks—and then there was this huge game of flag football. I'll spare you the details, but let's just say that the crazy kid, his goofy kid sister, and the girl with the used heart kicked everyone else's butts by several touchdowns. It's a weekend I won't soon forget.

When winter hit, it was difficult to find a way to see Rachel, but we talked almost every day. And for some reason she wanted to come to Stillwater for Christmas. And that's where, once again, my beautiful Texas girlfriend blew me away.

"ALEX, THERE'S SOMETHING I want you to help me with, and it's going to take more than just you and me."

"Sure Rachel, what do you want me to do?"

Two hours later, I was sitting with Rachel in my mom's car parked outside a dorm at the University of Tulsa.

"Are you going to tell me why we're here?"

Rachel shook her head.

"Nope. Remember that morning walk you took me on this fall?"

Oh, now I understood—it's called revenge, and it was Rachel's turn.

"Okay, fine, I'll wait. But remember I am your ride home."

Rachel gave me a "don't be a moron" look. And that's when I saw the face pressed against my window—it was Gus.

"Dude let me in. It's cold out here."

I unlocked the door and Gus—there was lot less of him now—climbed in the front seat.

"Alex, man it's good to see you."

I got a bone-cracking handshake.

"And Rachel . . . jeez, girl, you're looking hotter every day!"

Rachel blushed. Good ol' Gus, nice to know some things don't change. I smiled and gave him a high five.

"Glad to see you, too, man. How are you?"

"Great. I'm planning on graduating early and coming here for college, so I'm here this week to 'experience campus life,' " he said. "And I brought some friends."

I should have known: Trevor and JimBob.

"Hey, pardner, how in the heck are you?" the Idabel whiz kid greeted me with a killer smile, then tipped his Stetson (*yes, he was wearing a cowboy hat*) at Rachel.

"Ma'am. You're looking right beautiful today, Miss Rachel."

The guys climbed into the backseat of the car. Rachel told me to stay put, then she stepped out and opened the trunk. I felt a thunk. I opened my mouth to ask what was going on, then promptly shut it. I'd been told not to ask any questions.

"Hey!" Trevor said, as he settled in his seat. "Good to see ya'll."

I hollered out the window to Rachel: "So this is your help, huh? These are the other men in your life? These guys?"

"Don't underestimate them," she said. "They came through for me before. I trust 'em. Now, move over, because I'm driving."

She pushed me out of the way and slid behind the wheel. Moments later, the five of us slipped onto the icy streets of Tulsa.


"DO YOU EVEN KNOW where you're going?" We'd been driving for an hour now. And Tulsa late in the afternoon, on Christmas week, wasn't the best place in the world to be on the road.

Rachel patted my arm.

"Be patient," she said. "We're almost there. You guys in the back, ready?"

"Whenever you are Rachel," Trevor said.

Rachel turned the car down a narrow, tree-lined street and steered toward a huge gate. On the gate was a bronze Star of David.

We were at a . . . cemetery?

I looked at Rachel, wondering if she had lost her mind. She kissed me and gave me a reassuring look, as she pulled in and then gestured for me to get out of the car.

"I don't understand," I said.

"You will, Alex, I promise." Rachel headed into the cemetery.

We walked through a maze of tombstones toward a small area

surrounded by trees. I was pretty sure we were going to Kev's grave, but I didn't know why. Rachel was being mysterious, and, honestly, this wasn't something I'd associate with Christmas. You know, graveyards and stuff. Usually more Halloween fare in my experience.

"Okay, I know where we're going," I said, "but I still don't understand why we're here today."

"Just wait."

She waved at JimBob.

"Okay, guys we're ready."

My three friends walked toward us, each of them carrying a small cardboard box. Rachel directed them, like an orchestra's conductor, and soon, everyone stood in a circle around Kev's grave.

The stone read:

*"Kevin Gabriel Rubenstein*
*Beloved Son*
*Born April 18, 1991*
*Died October 27, 2007"*

Beneath those words, were some others in Hebrew.

Rachel reached inside her coat and brought out two long blue envelopes and several small, smooth stones. She laid one of the envelopes on Kev's tombstone and gave each of us a stone and everyone but me a box.

"According to Jewish tradition," she said, "the ultimate kindness and respect one can show a person who has died is to place a pebble or stone on his grave or tombstone."

Rachel placed her small smooth stone on the top of the marker on Kevin's grave.

"When you place stones on top of a gravestone, it's a sign that the deceased has not been forgotten."

She nodded, and Gus, JimBob, and Trevor each took their stones and, like she did, one by one placed them on top of the stone Rachel had laid. Then they opened their boxes and each removed a small piece of granite. JimBob put his on the ground to the right of Kev's tombstone. Gus sat his on top of that one, then Trevor did the same to Gus's. The pieces of granite formed a picture—an engraving of the drawing Kev had made of me and him standing outside of his cartoon studio.

"Alex, I wanted to do this to say thank you to Kevin. He saved my life. And while I know how painful this has been for you, I felt that, personally, I had never properly thanked him."

She handed me the second blue envelope.

"This is a copy of a letter I wrote to Kevin," she said. "The original will stay here with him. I sent another copy to his parents. I would like you to read it. I asked Gus, Trevor, and JimBob to help, because they're so important to me and to you. They stood with us when no one else would, so I felt they should be here today."

I didn't know how to respond. I rolled my stone in my hands. In all this time, I had never once been to Kev's grave. But today, here in the cold, winter Oklahoma air, well, it was okay to be here.

"I don't know what to say."

I looked at Rachel and then at Gus, Trevor, and JimBob.

"What I do know is Kev would have loved all of you. He'd have thought you guys were the best, because you are. You're all exactly yourself, and you taught me that I deserve to be that, too. And, well, he would have wanted all of you as friends."

Rachel pointed to the envelope.

"Why don't you read the letter?"

I opened the envelope and unfolded the blue paper.

Dear Kevin,

You and I have never met, but today we are as close as two friends can be. My name is Rachel Lynn Clark, and I'm seventeen. I live in Amarillo, Texas, with my family, and over the last year, I've come to know, and fall deeply in love with, your best friend, Alex Anderson.

I love Alex with everything I have, and, someday soon, I'm going to marry him. But I also love you. I love you because of your simple, unselfish gift to a stranger.

Kevin, if it weren't for you, I would not be standing here today. I would have never had the opportunity to meet Alex, or go to school, or compete in academic competitions. Without you, I would have died.

Because of your gift, your heart, I'm here. You gave everything you had to a total stranger. You saved my life. I can never repay you. I can never tell you in person how grateful I am. So I'm writing you this letter. I wanted to put down in words, how thankful I am.

And I wanted you to know how much I love Alex and how wonderful I think he is. Kevin, if there is a heaven—and I believe there is—then I know you're there. You deserve it because of everything you've done for the both of us.

And for that, I will, forever, remain your dear friend,

Rachel

I folded the letter and put it in my pocket. A cold mist had settled on the cemetery, and the sky had turned slate gray. Gus, Trevor, and JimBob slowly started walking back to the car.

I turned towards Kev's grave. The ice had formed a glaze on the small stones and Rachel's letter. The granite artwork had taken on the sheen of glass. I pulled Rachel against me and kissed her.

"Thank you," I said, "for making me come here."

Rachel gave me a little nod of understanding, then she also headed back to the car.

I stayed still, rooted to the spot, and, despite the cold, felt happy.

It was as if my life had come full circle: From the time I was little Kev had been my best friend. We'd shared secrets. We'd made plans. We'd gotten into trouble and we'd raced motorcycles. Kev had shared everything with me. But his greatest gift was leaning against my mom's car, shivering in her wool coat, pink sweater, and blue jeans.

"Thanks, Kev," I said. "You saved me, too."

I put my stone next to the stones of my friends on the tombstone. Then I turned and started for the car. I opened the passenger door and crawled inside.

Rachel shifted into drive and began to pull away from the curb, only to slam on the brakes and point back at Kev's grave.

"Alex? What . . . what's that?"

I looked up and saw it: There, on his tombstone, on top of the stone I had just placed, sat a small, sterling silver bracelet, with a heart that sparkled in the snow.

# About the Author

M. Scott Carter is an award-winning political reporter for The Journal Record, a photographer, and a magazine writer. *Stealing Kevin's Heart* is his debut young adult novel.

An Oklahoma native, Carter has been a contributing editor to *Oklahoma Today* magazine. His stories, essays, and photographs have also appeared in The Dallas Morning News, The St. Louis Post-Dispatch, The Kansas City Star, The Tulsa World, and the Boston Globe.

He lives with his wife, Karen, and their four children in Oklahoma City. Visit him at www.MScottCarter.com.